I0768624

An Enduring Romance Amid Civil Unrest

P. C. CHINICK

Russian Hill Press Book
United States • United Kingdom • Australia

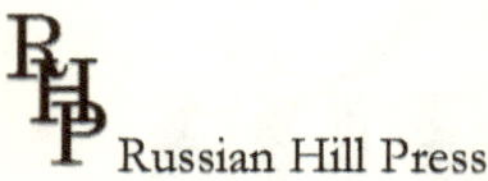
Russian Hill Press

ISBN: 979-8-9879285-6-1 (softcover)
ISBN: 979-8-9879285-7-8 (e-Book)

Library of Congress Control Number: 2024919855

Cover Designer: Tatiana Villa

RED ASSCHER SERIES

Living in Fear
Living in Turmoil
Living in War

Artic
Ocean
Bering Sea
Barents Sea
East Siberian
Sea
Anadyr
Murmansk
Laptev Sea
Kara Sea
Saint Petersburg
Arkhangelsk
Magadan
Moscow
Norilsk
Vyatka
Yakutsk
Crimea
RUSSIA
Perm
Black
Sea
Yekaterinburg
Omsk
Khabarovsh
Tayshet
Caspian Sea
Novonikolayevsk
Lake
Baikal
Irkutsk
Chita
Port Arthur
Vladivostok

ROMAN AND KIRA

ONE

Russia 1898

ROMAN PAVLOVITCH STRODE up the stone steps of the Russian Summer Palace. A pang struck his stomach like a bayonet had pierced it. He felt torn between an obligation to duty and a yearning for something he could not define. Roman hoped to make a quick appearance, dutifully complete his obligatory responsibilities, convey his apologies, and escape the evening's ceremonial trivialities. He returned the salute to a sentry who pushed open an elaborately carved door. It scraped across the floor with a sound as piercing as a screeching hawk. He stepped onto the Italian white Statuario marble foyer, a testament to the empire's grandeur. Roman tugged on his tunic, cleared his throat, inhaled, and slowly exhaled.

Melodic chamber music from the ballroom echoed through the hall. He entered an amber-hued area lit by candles in crystal chandeliers that hung from a gilded ceiling. Ladies bejeweled in scoop-necked gowns and gentlemen in formal black tailcoats or military uniforms laden with ribbons waltzed around the opulent room. Many of those not dancing admired their figures in the mirrored walls.

Roman approached the thrones of Tsar Nicholas II and Tsarina Alexandra. He bowed to each as a gesture of respect, then joined a lively group of fellow officers.

Debutantes from across the floor concealed their giddiness behind fluttering fans. Roman and his friends nudged one another like schoolboys. One officer dared another to request a dance. They all snickered and taunted the man.

Roman's laughter faded, and his body became rigid. A wave of uneasiness washed over him. A demure young strawberry-blonde in a short-sleeved light blue gown had captured his attention. Her curled tendrils bounced off her shoulders as she glided across the floor. She adjusted her white gloves at the elbows, then fidgeted with a modest jeweled necklace draped around her long, slender neck. He found himself unable to look away.

A smack on the back broke Roman's focus. A comrade shoved a glass of vodka into his hand. He lost sight of the maiden. He searched the room like a hungry lion, then spotted her amidst a crowd. Her grace and elegance as she greeted each guest captivated him. He thought she was a favorable interlude to the otherwise boorish affair. Roman watched her wend her way toward the terrace. He longed to know more about her. He gulped his drink to gain courage and followed her through the opened small-paned glass doors.

THE MAIDEN WALKED onto a moonlit stone terrace and inhaled a breath of spring air. A gentle breeze carried the fragrance of roses. She began to sway to the Strauss waltz. She watched a young couple walk along the garden path. An attentive chaperone mirrored their pace.

The maiden jumped at the deep voice with a soft and gentle lilt that spoke from behind. "The red rose whispers of passion, and the white rose breathes of love. O, the red rose is a falcon. And the white rose is a dove."

She turned and caught the sparkle in the stranger's hazel eyes. They were gentle eyes, not those of a predator. He was a tall, chiseled-jaw officer in his mid-twenties. She recognized the Imperial Guard uniform of a red tunic, blue britches, and high black boots. Numerous medals adorned his chest. "You're a poet, Sir."

He smiled as her green eyes peered over the top of her fan. "Not I, Mademoiselle, but rather an Irishman named O'Reilly."

"Which rose are you, red or white?"

"Your preference Mademoiselle. Allow me to introduce myself, Lieutenant Roman Pavlovitch." He clicked his heels and bowed.

She slapped her fan closed. "How impetuous of you—to announce yourself before we have been formally introduced." She allowed the corners of her mouth to tilt upward.

"I feared you might slip away before I had the chance to speak with you."

She waved off an older woman who stood at the terrace doorway.

"Your mother?"

"My aunt."

"Why have I never seen you before?" he said.

"I have not been to the palace since I was a child. My father has allowed me to accompany him for what is left of the season in St. Petersburg." She stepped forward. "I must return to my aunt."

"Your name, fair lady?"

She ignored his request and strolled past him, close enough to catch a hint of lavender mingled with horse sweat.

"Perhaps we shall meet again." Roman bowed.

"Perhaps." She slapped her fan.

ROMAN WALKED BACK into the palace. He spied his friends across the room and glared. They had lifted their glasses to him and laughed as the young woman walked away.

Uri, the tallest of the three, was a childhood friend. He and Roman had joined the guard together, their bond akin to brothers in arms. The other fellows were

Boris, the second son of a duke, and Fëdor, of no particular nobility, who had a nervous habit of chewing on his handlebar mustache. This diverse group all served together in the Chevalier Guard Regiment.

Roman joined his friends. "She wouldn't reveal her name."

"Lovely, is she not?" Boris said. "Her name is Kira Aleksandrovna. She's engaged to a prominent Colonel. Her father oversees the Belorussian government and has political ties with the Tsar."

Roman grabbed a coupe glass of champagne from a servant's tray, motioned for him to stay, downed one, and seized another. He watched Kira exit with her aunt.

"Easy old man. You know you can't hold your drink," Uri said.

Roman guzzled the second drink. He swayed a bit. Uri steadied him.

Fëdor said, "Did you see that degenerate who approached the royal carriage today? A few slashes to his face with my sword put that socialist pig in his place."

"Yes, but you almost fell off your horse in the process." The men laughed, except for Roman.

"These peasants are too bold," Boris said. "These serfs were freed from their landowners and allowed to purchase farms. They ought to be be toiling in their fields, not staging demonstrations."

"They must sell everything they produce to pay

their taxes." Roman's cheeks reddened. "How is it that we allow our people to starve?"

Uri squeezed his arm and shook his head. "Not here, Roman. You know the situation is delicate."

Fëdor twisted his mustache. Roman believed he grew it to camouflage his youthful looks.

Boris shifted his weight and stared at Roman.

"Maybe we should go somewhere with less prying ears," Uri said. "Boris, you and Fëdor go find young ladies to dance with while I take Roman outside."

"I'm fine." Roman shook off Uri's grip. He and Uri stood in the same spot that Kira had been moments before. The scent of her perfume still lingered.

"Take care around Boris. Remember he is part of the aristocracy," Uri said.

Kira's heart-shaped face appeared before Roman. "I need to find her."

"And do what?"

"I don't know." Roman stared into the distance. "But I must speak with her again."

"I sense a sea of troubles."

KIRA WALKED WITH her aunt to the waiting carriage, her mind a whirlwind of conflicting emotions. A tingle ran through her body as she thought about her encounter with the lieutenant. *He is handsome but a bit brazen.* Her lips formed a smile as her chin tipped. She sensed her aunt monitoring her.

"What are you thinking about my dear?"

"It was a lovely evening wasn't it, Auntie."

"It's too bad your fiancé could not join us tonight."

"Yes, too bad."

TWO

The sun hung high over a cloudless late afternoon sky. Roman mulled over his new orders to escort out-of-town guests. He wiped his brow and sighed. *I'd rather face a bullet head-on than safeguard aristocrats.*

Roman mounted his Trakehner gelding, Ivan. At 16 hands, he was a magnificent equine with a long, silky black mane and shiny chestnut coat. He trotted through a neighborhood of grand mansions with their groomed gardens and the absence of piled-high garbage found in less affluent areas. Roman surveyed parents strolling the promenade, holding their children's hands. A stark contrast to his status as a soldier without ties to his own legacy.

They passed a coach as the driver whipped his horse. Ivan's ears pulled back; he shook his head and snorted a whinny. "Easy boy." Roman patted the Ivan's neck. He had raised the gelding from a colt.

They had been through several uprisings that had taken them far from home. On one occasion, he ordered a field surgeon to remove a bullet that Ivan had received in battle. He still bore the scar on his left hindquarter.

Roman pulled on Ivan's reins and stopped in front of a majestic brick three-story terrace house. Two dominant snow-white Arabians were hitched to an open carriage, their coats radiated a pink shimmer. The coachman climbed the stoop of the mansion and knocked on the door. A stocky older man exited. He wore a long black coat that hung below his knees and a top hat. He stuffed a cane under his arm and pulled on his gloves. A young woman wearing a full-length light gray coat with sleeves that puffed out at the upper arm and tapering around the wrists accompanied him. Exotic feathers adorned her headpiece.

Roman's stomach tightened. His mind flashed back to the moonlit terrace and the waltz that had been playing. The woman stepped into the carriage. Their eyes met before she sat. Puzzlement crossed her face; then her lips slowly formed a smile.

"Good day, Lieutenant," Kira said. Her father swiveled to see the officer.

Roman tipped his helmet with a slight bow.

Alexander Aleksandrovich frowned at his daughter. He tapped his cane on the floor and ordered the carriage to move ahead. "Who is that man, Kira?"

"Oh, someone who attended the gala last evening."

Roman remained close behind the carriage. A

slight grin arose. He diverted his focus to the street corner ahead. An unkempt man dressed in rags looked out of place. Without hesitation, he yelled at the coachman, "Whip the horses and move out." Roman dug his heels into Ivan and galloped toward the vagabond. The man tried to weave past him, but Roman cut him off with a drawn saber before the man could reach the carriage. The vagrant removed a cylindrical object from under his coat. Roman pulled hard on Ivan's reins. The horse reared up, causing the man to drop the object. The man lost his footing on loose stones and fell on top of it. Roman turned Ivan away moments before the device exploded under the assassin.

Roman raced ahead to catch the carriage. He grabbed the reins of one horse and gradually slowed them to a walk. He saw Kira wrapped in her father's arms. The speed of the ride had caused both their hats to fly off. Her hair lay in tangles along her back. Tears trickled down her cheeks as she turned to him and mouthed, "Thank you."

At that moment, he knew he had surrendered his heart.

Kira had persuaded her father to invite Roman as the guest of honor that evening. The stuffy protocol caused Roman to fidget in his seat. But he was willing to suffer for the opportunity to sit at Kira's side.

Elegantly dressed ladies and gentlemen sat around

a long dining table, which was lit by candelabras. A multitude of tableware and wine goblets graced each place setting. White-clad servants served the first course of borscht with a dollop of *crème fraîche*.

"That was a heroic feat you performed, Lieutenant," an older woman spoke out.

The man beside her said, "I don't know what we are going to do with these emboldened kulaks."

"Maybe we could reduce their taxes so they can feed their families," Roman said. The room fell quiet. All heads turned. A few leaned forward to get a better look at him.

Someone at the far end of the table spoke, "What if we take our plates out into the streets and stoke their bellies." Everyone laughed except Roman. Kira glanced at her father.

Roman used the excuse of reaching for his glass of wine to touch Kira's bare arm. He felt his pulse race and was pleased when she did not pull back. Kira's aunt across the table gave them a stern look that caused Kira to blush.

A guest cleared his throat and said, "Alexander, when do you plan to leave for Moscow?"

"In a few days."

Kira's green eyes held a sadness that crept over Roman. He placed the wine goblet down.

"Maybe you should take the young lieutenant," another said. "Given the unrest many of us could benefit from such protection."

Alexander said, "Um. We shall see."

Kira squeezed Roman's forearm under the table. He remained poised. He rested his hand on hers, then interlaced his fingers with hers. Roman believed he heard a coo escape Kira's lips.

ROMAN ENTERED HIS shared quarters with thoughts of Kira. He found Uri lying on his bed reading. He looked up from his book. "I heard you ran into a little scuffle."

Roman plopped onto an overstuffed chair. "It was nothing." He swung his leg over the armrest and began to hum.

"I heard that you were invited for supper at the Aleksandrovich's residence."

Roman produced an impish grin.

Uri sat upright. "Have you lost your head?" He sprang to his feet and placed his hands on his hips. "What are you doing? She is engaged."

"Maybe." He shrugged. "But she's not married, not yet anyway." Roman rose, grabbed his valet bag off the highboy, and headed down the hall.

Uri yelled after him, "You know you're crazy."

THREE

ANTICIPATION SWELLED WITHIN Kira, reminiscent of a crescendo in a symphony. She spotted Roman dismount his horse and approach along the pebbled path. Her legs trembled beneath her dress like an excited child waiting for a sweet. Her face flushed as she spoke. "Lieutenant Pavlovitch, you remember Countess Maria Protasova Sheremeteva from last evening. Masha is my dearest and favorite aunt."

Roman bowed at the waist to acknowledge his station.

"Father is in meetings all day, so I have invited the Lieutenant to ride with us." Kira caught her aunt's raised eyebrow. She returned a smile.

The Countess eyed the lieutenant. "I have had a lunch packed. There should be enough for all."

A groomsman assisted Kira onto her horse. She placed her leg over the horn of the sidesaddle, then fitted the twill tape sewn inside her skirt over her boot instep to ensure that her leg remained covered while riding. She secured the hat's veil around her chin to protect her from insects.

"The Countess believes it to be undignified for a woman to sit atop a horse," Kira said as she tried to cloak her laughter. Masha waved off the driver, grabbed the reins of the two-wheel horse carriage, and drove off.

Kira sat upright in her saddle and addressed Roman. "You resemble a Reynold's painting in your uniform atop your steed." He looked away, but she caught his cheeks flush.

They cantered across the estate's meadow, bordered by tall leafy trees. A minor sprinkle earlier that morning provided a fresh airing of sweet wildflowers and the mustiness of grasses.

Kira noticed that Masha had fallen less than a respectful distance behind. She slowed the horse to a walk. Roman reined in his horse to match her pace.

"Last evening you were rather rude in your remark that we mistreat the peasantry," Kira said.

"Was I?" Roman ignored her gaze and kept his focus ahead.

"Do you have a kinship with these people?"

He halted Ivan and turned to her. "It's not that I support insolence, but if wealth were broadly allocated wisely, uprisings might be lessened and the country less turbulent."

"But how would the aristocracy live? You know,

they support your livelihood too."

"I'm only saying conditions might be better if properly managed."

"Please don't speak of these matters in front of my father."

"As you wish."

Silence settled over them.

The uncomfortable silence led Kira to speak. "How did you come to be an Imperial Guard?"

He stiffened as if addressing an officer. "It's in our blood. Several Pavlovitch generations have proudly served Tsars. My grandfather saved Alexander II from an assassination."

"As you did for my father and me. I am forever in your debt." She held a steady gaze into his warm hazel eyes and wondered how his full lips might feel against hers.

"You said that you haven't been to St. Petersburg since childhood."

Kira was startled back to reality by the sound of Roman's voice. "What?"

"Where do you reside, when you're not attending cotillions?"

"I live with my family in Minsk." She found it difficult to ignore his lean body with broad shoulders and narrow hips.

Roman turned his head away and righted himself in the saddle.

Kira pointed to a knoll laced with yellow, cream,

and a hint of amethyst wildflowers that descended to a bend in the river. "This looks the perfect place."

Puzzlement crossed his face.

"For a picnic." She dropped the reins and raised her arms. "Please assist me."

Roman dismounted and reached for Kira, who slid into his arms. They stood for a moment in an embrace until they heard a loud clearing of Masha's throat. They immediately separated. Masha scowled at Kira as she handed her a wool blanket. Roman picked up the food basket and hauled it to an idyllic spot Kira had chosen under the canopy of an immense oak.

Masha opened the basket, pulled out a bottle of champagne, and handed it to Roman. He wrestled with the cork. It popped and flew by Kira's head. Bubbles overflowed from the mouth of the bottle.

"Grab a glass, Kira," Masha said. "We must save every precious drop."

Kira laid out platters of cheeses, cold meats, bread, fruit, and blinchiki, a sweet pastry filled with cottage cheese and honey. She served a plate for her aunt and one for Roman before serving herself.

Kira's horse whinnied. "I think my mare is smitten with your stallion."

"It won't do her any good. He's a gelding."

Kira tilted her head to one side and furrowed her brow. Masha placed her serviette over her mouth to conceal her laughter.

After eating, Masha reclined against the tree, her

eyes closed in a peaceful slumber. Kira placed a finger to her lips and motioned for Roman to rise. They quietly slipped away to the secluded river's edge.

Roman boldly took Kira's right hand.

His touch sent a jolt of electricity through her. This new sensation, thrilling and terrifying, left her yearning for more.

He immediately released his hold. "Forgive me. It is wrong of me."

"I don't understand."

"The ring. I felt your engagement ring."

Kira sighed. "It's my father's wish, not mine. I have only met the man once and … well … he is old and fat and smells of spirits. I do not care for him in the least."

"Nevertheless, you are engaged."

"But if only …"

In the distance, Masha yelled. "It's time we head back. Your father will be waiting."

ROMAN LED IVAN into the stable. He saw Boris rubbing liniment on his horse and approached. "How can someone withdraw from an engagement without embarrassment?"

"Don't be a fool." Boris continued to groom his horse.

"I need your help."

"If you follow that path and fail, you will not be able to recant. Your reputation will be ruined and your commission stripped."

Roman leaned against the stall and nodded.

"The main objective of these marriages is to increase property or wealth. And Kira's father possesses an abundance of the former. Your only recourse is to discover financial impropriety."

"Can this be accomplished in a clandestine manner as to not embarrass anyone?"

"I can't promise, but I will speak with my uncle. He has a few connections. Maybe he can discover something useful. In the meantime, you need to ingratiate yourself into the family."

FOUR

At Kira's invitation, Roman returned to the estate for an afternoon social gathering. He spotted a white rose pinned above Kira's ear. His heart pounded with excitement, knowing it symbolized the poem he had recited to her. It had been over a week since the picnic when they last saw each other. He followed Kira as she raised the hem of her dress, exposing layers of petticoats. She accompanied her father down the stone steps to the garden.

Tables and chairs dotted the lawn in intimate settings. White-gloved servants meandered with trays of champagne and vodka. A few meters away, men and women practiced archery; some played croquet while others strolled through the gardens. Men tipped their toppers and straw hats as ladies passed. Women twirled colorful parasols that protected their faces from the heat of the day.

Roman watched Kira excuse herself from her father and wander beside him.

"Why are you staring at me like that?" she said.

"I approve of the rose."

She tilted her head with a coy smile and fluttered her fan. "Will you walk with me?"

Tall leafy trees, surrounded by a ground cover bouquet of ornamental snowballs of white and pink perennials, lined one side of the pebbled walkway. On the other side, a narrow, multi-tiered artificial waterfall percolated. Roman remained on the outer edge to protect Kira from the water spray.

Roman was at a loss for something to say, then blurted. "Beautiful day." He felt his cheeks burn at the ridiculous comment. *Just tell her how you feel.*

"It's a perfect day." She rested her hand on his forearm.

Roman noticed that she was not wearing her ring. The nagging pit in his stomach subsided.

"Father used the liniment oil that you sent over for his rheumatism. How did you know about such a cure?"

"I noticed that he continually rubbed his hands at dinner the other evening. After a hard workout with Ivan, I rub liniment on his legs to reduce muscle soreness. After using it for years I find that my hands are less stiff."

"He is very grateful."

"Your father says he will no longer require my services."

Kira remained silent.

They entered a canopy of purple wisteria that engulfed a trellis and hid them from meddlesome eyes.

Roman seized the isolation to stroke her cheek. Her skin felt softer than a rose petal. She leaned into his hand. The sensation of warm water raced through his body. He lowered his head and pressed his lips onto hers.

A bird rustled in the wisteria, making him aware of his surroundings. Kira broke away. "We mustn't."

He gently took her arm and drew her in. She nuzzled her forehead on his chest. "I'm promised to another."

"I know." He lifted her head and cupped her chin in his hand.

She gazed at him with sadness. "We leave for Moscow the day after tomorrow."

"Do you love me?" he said.

"Wedding plans have been arranged."

"Do you love me?"

"My father is insistent."

"Do you love me?"

"I don't want to die without having lived." Her thoughts lingered in his eyes. "Yes. I love you."

He brushed a stray hair away from her cheek. "Trust me, everything will be set right."

FIVE

KIRA REFUSED HER father's hand. She refused to address him as she stepped out of the carriage. Her defiance shadowed him through the gothic archway of the clock tower at the train station. A jingling of a light rain drummed atop the metal roof. A scowl remained prominent while her father exchanged future-dated tickets for space on the 9:00 a.m. train to Moscow.

Alexander led his daughter onto the train platform. He opened the railroad car door and ushered Kira inside. The small private compartment held two red leather seat benches that faced each other. The porter placed their bags in the overhead rack. Alexander handed the man a few coins. Kira perched herself, cross-armed, and scrunched tight against the window as far away from her father as the compartment allowed.

Her mind slipped back to the argument they had

exchanged earlier that morning.

"I don't care if you hold your breath until you faint." Alexander's voice thundered and he slammed his fist on the desk. "You were spotted at the garden party in an embrace. What would your fiancé say if he found out about your scandalous behavior?"

"I don't care. I don't love him." Kira sat back in her chair, red-faced. *Thank God he hadn't heard about the kiss, or he would have sent me packing home to Mother in Minsk.* She touched her bottom lip. Roman's taste still lingered.

Alexander's voice softened. "You will learn to love Colonel Vershinin."

Kira remembered meeting Vershinin for the first time. She had been irritated by his overbearing manner—reminiscent of her father. "Oh … Oh … you're just too old to remember what it is to love."

"Kira …" he paused. "You have been groomed for this position since you were fifteen. This is no longer up for discussion."

The train lurched forward bringing her senses to the present moment.

Alexander opened a box of Zhorzh Borman chocolates, each sealed in a golden wrapper with the imperial coat of arms. Kira turned her nose in the air when he offered her one. He unwrapped the sweet, bit down, and slurped out the soft, gooey chocolate center.

I want to smash that sweet all over his face.

"Delicious," he said. "Your mother would be jealous."

Kira stared out the window, vowing never to speak to him. She thought about making her escape, but where … Auntie Masha.

The train began to gain speed. *I still have time.* She slid her hand toward the door. Her fingers inched toward the handle.

Alexander said, "It's going to be a long trip if you refuse to speak,"

Kira withdrew her reach and leaned back in her seat. She saw the silhouette of a man race onto the platform, but the distance was too far for her to identify him. Her anger subsided to anguish and disappointment. Her heart ached to know what Roman was doing at that moment.

"URI, GET PACKED. We're going to Moscow." Roman led Ivan into the stable and opened the door to his stall, where a fresh layer of straw and pine shavings had been spread on the floor.

Uri stopped polishing his boots. "Why?"

Roman picked up a brush and wiped down Ivan. "I went to speak with Kira this morning, but a servant told me she and her father had left for Moscow. I know he is trying to keep us apart." Roman secured a stable blanket on Ivan, then poured oats into his trough. "I raced to reach her, but the train was pulling out."

"Your pursuit is reckless." Uri rose from the bale

of hay he had been sitting on. "Her father has power. His leverage could have you demoted or worse discharged. Don't forget you're up for a promotion that will elevate your status. Why take the chance?"

Roman replied, "I've already arranged for all four of us to leave on the next train to Moscow."

"Why drag the others into this?"

"Drag who?" Boris said as he and Fëdor entered the stable.

"Roman wants us to risk our careers to go after a woman," Uri said.

"Who's the woman?" Fëdor raised an eyebrow.

"You remember. A while back at the palace," Boris said. "The beauty that bewitched his senses."

"Oh, yea." Fëdor chewed on his mustache.

"I heard you mention Moscow," Boris said. "I have an uncle who lives there. He is intimate with the same circle as Kira's aunt, the Countess. He might be willing to help us."

Roman's brow puckered.

"Plant a seed of debauchery within her circle," Boris said.

"Debauchery?" Fëdor said. "How exciting."

"Boris." Uri shook his head. "Don't encourage either of them."

"Look, you are my closest friends and I need your help," Roman said. "I need Boris because of his contacts. I need you, Uri, to help me avoid losing my commission. And you." Roman laid his hand on

Fëdor's shoulder. "I need you most of all. To find us a good tavern." He winked at the others.

Fëdor spoke up first. "I'll go."

"Count me in," Boris replied.

Uri rolled his eyes. "All right, but let's try and keep our wits about us and avoid doing anything foolish."

Roman stretched his arm with his palm down. Each man laid his hand on top of the others. "Let us rescue a maiden," Roman said.

In unison, they repeated, "Let us rescue a maiden."

SIX

KIRA STOOD NEXT to the picture window in the family's Moscow apartment. Gray clouds masked any sign of a morning sun. The cobbled street below serviced horseless carriages along with a motored carriage. *What a funny-looking contraption.* The impatient driver beeped his horn several times, but the coachman ignored him. Kira smiled, amused by the man's defiance.

Her smile faded when she spotted a cavalry soldier approach dressed in a red tunic and black pants, reminiscent of Roman's uniform. Kira tightly gripped the back of a chair to steady herself. The soldier and horse moved closer. Her heart beat faster with anticipation. He veered his horse toward the hitching post in front of their door. *Is he going to stop and dismount?* She dug her nails into the chair. A tilbury carriage passed. The officer tipped his cap to the occupants inside and continued along the street. Kira relaxed her stance and exhaled. Her head hung, and a deep sigh escaped her lips.

Alexander took a sip of coffee and placed his cup on the table beside him. "What are your plans today?" He relaxed on a gold and white striped empire-style chaise.

Kira ignored his words, retaining her vow never to speak to her father. She walked with determination, causing her heels to vehemently clack against the black onyx marble floor. She plopped herself on an ornately carved chair, grabbed a book, and flipped through the pages.

"I received an invitation to a ball." Alexander waved the letter at her. "But if you are not speaking to me, I guess I'll have to decline." He rested his head on the padded rollback and swung his legs onto the end of the chaise. "I've invited Colonel Mikhail Vershinin to join us for dinner tonight."

Kira slammed the book shut with a resounding thud. "I don't want him here. I don't want to see him. And I definitely don't want to marry him. Her words boomed with a defiance that reverberated through the room.

Alexander leaped to his feet. "You will do as instructed, young lady. This arrangement was agreed upon years ago and his wealth will suit you very well." He paced the floor. "We shall see what your mother has to say about this matter."

Kira sensed her throat tighten as she bristled with anger. She felt as through her body would explode from all extremities. Knowing her station and that she could not win the argument, she rose and rushed out of the room in tears. Her sobs echoed through the corridor.

KIRA PEERED DOWN from the top of the stairs to see Colonel Mikhail Vershinin standing in the foyer. Her memory did not recall him as a stout man with a scruffy beard and pyramid mustache. The Colonel wore a dark blue high-collared double-breasted tunic with a thin belt cinched around his fat belly and straight-legged trousers.

"Daughter." Her father waved. "Come and welcome your fiancé."

Kira descended, taking a moment at each step with thoughts of feigning an illness. The closer she got, the more repulsed she became at the sight of his puffy eyes and nose too small for his face. Mikhail clicked his heels, bowed, and kissed her hand. Kira pulled away before he had a chance to right himself. She spotted her father's frown but disregarded it.

"How lovely you look, my dear," Mikhail said.

Kira rendered a polite smile.

The trio retired to a pastel drawing room with an ornate ceiling and heavily embossed wall covering. Kira sat on a chair rather than the settee to avoid Mikhail sitting next to her. Alexander nodded to a white-clad servant who held a tray of food and drink.

"How have you been, Mikhail?" Alexander said.

Mikhail plunked onto the chaise and took a cup of tea and some sweets from the gloved servant. "It is difficult these days with the street skirmishes and peasant revolts." He pushed a petit four into his mouth and continued, "There is even talk that Japan might be stirring up something ..." He swallowed, licked his fingers, and continued. "At Port Arthur."

"I hope that doesn't mean war."

"We shall see." Mikhail slurped his tea.

"What we need is a celebration," Alexander said. "The union between you and my daughter is long overdue."

A sudden cold clamminess prickled across Kira's skin.

"Yes, a wedding." Mikhail brought his hands together with a clap. "When?"

Kira's jaw tightened. She struggled to maintain composure even though her hands trembled.

"Within a few weeks," Alexander said.

Kira shot her father a fierce look like a wild cat ready to pounce.

He continued, "It will be June and the weather in Moscow will be suitable for an outdoor reception."

"But, Papa." Kira's voice was thick with emotion. "What about Mama? She can't possibly be here in time to help with all the preparations and I won't marry without her presence."

"I wired your mother before we left St. Petersburg. She and the family should be here within days."

Kira's stomach clenched. She was utterly helpless, like a butterfly ready to have its wings pinned and mounted in a display box. She stared at the religious icon hanging on the wall. It was Mary holding baby Jesus in her arms. *Oh, Mother of God, please deliver me from this suffering.*

SEVEN

The only accommodations the musketeers, as the four called themselves, found in Moscow were less than desirable. The dimly lit tavern, nestled in a narrow alleyway, had candle-soot-stained walls, and the air smelled of curdled sour mash. The wooden table and chairs were worn and splintered, and the floor was covered in a layer of sawdust. Roman sat with his wool coat wrapped tight. He propped his feet on a wooden chair before an empty fireplace. Their room one flight up was in no better condition.

Fëdor slammed an empty glass on the stained table and refilled it with vodka. "Where are Uri and Boris?"

"Relax." Roman yawned. "Boris has gone to visit his wealthy uncle. Uri—well, you know where he is."

"It's remarkable. That guy knows every gambling house in every town." Fëdor gulped his vodka.

The tavern door opened, exposing what light was

left of the day. A number of hungover customers moaned. Boris pulled up a chair and plopped beside Roman. "My uncle said there is a grand ball tomorrow. Kira is certain to be there. I procured invitations for us."

"What makes you think we'll find her at the ball?" Fëdor said.

"What else is there for the aristocracy to do in Moscow?" Roman said.

The door opened again, and further moans erupted from the crowd. Uri stumbled in along with a stout man dressed in civilian clothes. "Guess who I found," Uri slurred his words. The intoxicated men propped themselves against each other for support.

"Where the hell did you find him?" Boris turned up his nose.

"Cards." Uri laughed. "I've never seen anyone lose so much money at one time. I know a secret." Uri put his finger to his lips and whispered loudly, "He's getting married in a few days to the lovely Kira Aleksandrovna. This fine fellow is Colonel Mikhail Vershinin."

Roman sat upright, curled his upper lip, and gave Vershinin a hard stare that could cut a diamond.

The Colonel tried to click his heels and bow but instead fell forward. Roman rose and caught him, and placed him in a chair. The sight of this drunken man slumped, his jaw slacked and pressed against his chest, left an acid taste in Roman's mouth. "Uri, take Vershinin to the room. Fëdor, show them the way."

"What are you going to do, Roman?" Boris said.

Roman remained fixed on Vershinin as Uri assisted the lumbering drunk up the stairs. "I don't know, Boris—I just don't know."

ROMAN, BORIS, AND Fёdor ate a breakfast of porridge and washed it down with coffee. The reverberation of clomp, clomp, clomp informed them that Uri and Vershinin were making their way downstairs. Vershinin plunked into a chair with a grunt. Roman glared at the bloated, red-eyed beast with disgust. Uri's appearance was less than worse for the wear. Boris and Fedor shifted uncomfortably in their seats.

Vershinin slammed his fist on the table and demanded vodka from the server. Uri covered his ears. "Must you be so boisterous?"

"Coffee might be better," Boris said.

Vershinin expelled a forceful grunt and shook his head. Roman smelled the odious odor that oozed from his body and the sour stench that spewed from each belch. The server placed a bottle and glass on the table. Vershinin grabbed it and poured a shot, spilling most of it, then lifted the shaking glass to his lips and gulped it. "Ah." His eyes widened. He looked around. "And who might you all be?"

Boris and Fёdor introduced themselves, while Roman remained silent.

Vershinin faced Roman. "Sir, have you a name?"

Roman clenched his fist. "Lieutenant Roman Pavlovitch."

"I too am an officer. Colonel Vershinin." He downed another shot.

"A disgraceful one," Roman muttered.

Boris elbowed Roman.

Roman knitted his brow and shrugged with disregard.

"Gentlemen," Vershinin rose. "I must be on my way. I have an engagement with my fiancé."

Roman pulled the Colonel back into his seat. "What's the rush? Have a drink." He filled the glass.

Uri slapped him on the back. "Yes, we've recently become good friends."

Vershinin thought for a moment, then downed the shot.

Roman whispered into Boris's ear. "Keep him drinking. See if there's a game going on in the back."

"Where are you going?"

"Don't let him leave." Roman left the tavern.

A WHITE-GLOVED man dressed in a black morning coat opened an elaborately carved wooden door. "Please announce to the Countess that Lieutenant Roman Pavlovitch needs to speak with her about an urgent matter."

The butler remained silent and stared at him with a blank expression.

Roman raised his voice. "Did you hear me, man? I must speak with the Countess."

A voice echoed from the hall. "Who is it, Petrov?"

Petrov kept watch over Roman when he answered. "A Lieutenant, Madam. He seems distressed."

The Countess appeared from around the corner. "Oh, it's you."

Roman bowed. "I'm sorry to disturb you Madam, but …"

"Yes, yes. What's this about?"

Roman hesitated. He glanced at Petrov, then at the Countess.

"It's all right. You can speak."

"It's about Colonel Vershinin."

"You better come in."

EIGHT

KIRA TUGGED AT the sides of her gown. "Auntie Masha, I think this needs a different sash." Before the Countess responded, a woman in a flowing yellow silk chiffon evening dress sauntered in. Kira's eyes widened, and her jaw dropped at the reflection in the full-length mirror. "Mother." She spun around with arms outstretched, but the sight of a furrowed brow and jutted jaw stopped her from rushing into her mother's arms.

"I understand there was trouble in St. Petersburg," her mother said.

Kira felt her cheeks flush and suppressed the urge to escape into the armoire. "You mean the attempt on our lives?" She entwined her fingers nervously, then returned to the mirror and adjusted her gown. She knew her mother referred to the gossip about her and

Roman at the garden party.

"You know exactly what I mean, young lady." The woman's face relaxed.

"Sister," the Countess said. Her voice carried a hint of displeasure.

Kira's mother dismissed her interruption with a wave of her hand. "Although, I am grateful for you and your father's well-being. Your father and I have cultivated this union to see that your station in life is well situated. To marry into the Romanov family would give you …"

"You mean your position, Mother."

"Don't be impertinent, young lady." She crossed the dressing room and gently placed her hands upon her daughter's shoulders. She spoke to the reflection in the mirror. "Your engagement has been arranged for years. To alter plans now would cause severe embarrassment to our family and compromise your father's political position. You know our dream is to return to St. Petersburg."

"Sister," the Countess interrupted. "Remember my situation? I entered into a loveless marriage with a man much older than myself. You know the hardships I faced. I still bear some of the scars. My only salvation was a stampede from a runaway carriage that freed me," she paused. "I have it on good authority that Colonel Vershinin is not the man for your daughter. Besides his age, he is too coarse for her youthful spirit."

Kira gave her aunt an appreciative nod.

"Maria, Kira is my daughter. I know what is appropriate."

"Mother, I understand my duty, but you need to accept that I … without purpose … fell in love with the lieutenant." Kira hesitated to speak Roman's name for fear of another reprimand from her mother.

"I want the finest for you. You are a shrewd, intelligent, and sensible woman." Her mother turned Kira around. "This is your obligation as my daughter." Kira threw her arms around her mother's neck, buried her face in her breast, and sobbed.

"Now, now. Wipe your tears. We are expecting guests along with your fiancé. You don't want him to see you with puffy red eyes."

"He won't be sober enough to notice." the Countess muttered.

"What was that, Sister?"

"Nothing."

Kira took the handkerchief from her mother, dabbed her eyes, and watched her mother exit the room.

"Oh Masha, what am I going to do?"

"Your mother might be headstrong but she is also fair. Remain stalwart. Time has a way of working things out."

NINE

1899

THE BALLROOM LACKED the elegance of a royal place. The walls were lined with textured paper, not mirrors, and the Tsar and Tsarina would not be in attendance. Those present deemed it a minor affair, yet it held a certain allure. A mixture of perfumes filled the air as hundreds of aristocrats crowded the room in their theatrical glamor.

Alexander Aleksandrovich brought the lively music to a sudden halt with a wave of his arm. "Ladies and Gentlemen." Crystal glasses pinged until the voices stilled. Lady Aleksandrovna stood beside her husband. "Ladies and Gentlemen, thank you all for witnessing this auspicious occasion. Her Ladyship and I are pleased to announce the wedding of our daughter Kira Maria Valentina Aleksandrovna and Colonel

Mikhail Vershinin." The guests erupted into cheers. Alexander motioned for them to restrain their enthusiastic applause. "The wedding will take place a month from today. Invitations to go out immediately. We wish the happy couple a happy life." He raised his champagne glass. "*Nastorvia!*"

Kira picked at the ruffles that ran the length of her lavender crepe gown. She adjusted the coal-black sash cinched tight around her tapered waist, which accented her hourglass figure. Vershinin, in a dress uniform with epaulets and a dozen medals pinned on his chest, took Kira's arm. He parted the crowd, congratulations of applause and hurrahs erupted from guests. Vershinin attempted to strut like a peacock boasting a colorful plumage. Instead, he wobbled like a penguin. Kira hung her head. Her sympathy was not for him but for herself.

Roman stood against the back wall and refused to toast. He put down his drink and recalled his first meeting with the Colonel. The grotesque fat man had collapsed in a drunken stupor at the tavern. Roman's jaw tightened, and he let out a quiet growl.

Kira's angelic rose-blushed face lifted. Her eyes caught his. Roman wanted to take her in his arms and once again feel her soft lips upon his. He took a step in her direction.

Fëdor and Uri each grabbed an arm. "Steady, old man."

The music began. Couples two-stepped around

the ballroom. Boris had just arrived and sidled next to Roman. "You look as pale as a cadaver." Boris looked at the others. "What's happened?"

"Kira's wedding date was announced," Uri said. "Where have you been?"

"Speaking with my uncle," Boris said. "He claims that the Colonel is heavily in debt. The Tsar has been giving him money out of the royal coffers. However, that's about to come to an end. He needs this union to acquire a steady income. In exchange, the Alesksandrovich's will receive a place at court."

Roman raised a brow. "That is useful infor-mation." He watched Vershinin stagger over with Kira in tow.

"Good evening, gentlemen," Vershinin rocked back on his heels. "Let me present my fiancé, Kira Aleksandrovna. I met these fine officers the other evening."

Roman gave a slight bow. "How are you, Miss Aleksandrovna?"

"I am well, Lieutenant Pavlovitch," Kira said.

"You two have met?"

Roman kept his focus on Kira as he spoke to Vershinin. "I had the pleasure of escorting Miss Aleksandrovna and her father while they were in St. Petersburg."

"I see … and what brings you to Moscow?"

Roman saw Kira tense up.

Boris stepped in. "We are here to speak with my

uncle on important business."

Roman nodded, grateful for Boris's lie.

"We thought it our duty to attend the ball and bestow our accessibility on the lovely ladies of Moscow." Uri smiled at Kira.

"Yes, these Muscovites are quite fair." Fëdor twirled his mustache and scanned the room.

The orchestra changed the tempo. Roman's mind flashed back to the palace terrace in St. Petersburg, where they first met. They had played the same, Strauss Waltz. "Colonel, would you do me the honor of allowing me a dance with your fiancé?"

Vershinin's eyes narrowed, but he nodded. Roman placed his left hand on Kira's back, placed her gloved hand in his right, and they waltzed away.

"I was afraid to ask in front of Vershinin," Kira said. "Where did you meet him?"

"Uri met him the other night." Roman refrained from revealing more.

"He's watching us," she said, her voice quivering with discomfort.

"He doesn't care for the way you are looking at me." He smiled.

"I can't help myself." Her cheeks were in full bloom, void of embarrassment.

The music ended, but Roman held on to Kira's arm. "He's coming over and the expression on his face is not pleasant," Roman said.

"You appear to be more than friends." Vershinin's

tenor was strained. "What's so amusing?"

Roman smiled. "I reminded Miss Aleksandrovna of the time my horse almost kicked her father."

Vershinin grunted. "Kira, I think it's time we return to the family." Kira looked across the room to see a stern expression in her father's eyes and a wrinkled brow on her mother. Vershinin clutched Kira's upper arm and yanked her away.

"That's no way to treat a lady."

Vershinin turned to Roman. "This is not your concern."

"I loathe seeing a woman, especially Miss Aleksandrovna, mistreated."

Vershinin dropped Kira's arm and closed in on Roman. "Sir, you are too attentive toward my fiancé."

Roman smelled his foul breath of liquor and decayed teeth.

"Gentlemen. Gentlemen." Alexander positioned himself between the fighting men. "Restrain yourselves." His voice turned harsh. "Kira, your mother is asking for you."

"But, Papa." His cold, blank stare caused her to turn on her heels. She passed Uri and Boris. "Protect him," she whispered.

"I better not hear of any ill-treatment of the young lady," Roman said as Uri tried to drag him away.

Vershinin freed himself from Alexander's hold. "I am going to let that go since we are friends."

"We are not friends." Roman eyed the man. "My

friend brought you around the other night to show me what a blackguard you are."

"You had better watch your step …"

"Or what?"

"I have restrained from the gossip about you and my fiancé, but I fear at this juncture I can no longer sit idle." Vershinin stopped for a moment. "It is time for action."

"Agreed," Roman said.

"I challenge you to a pistol duel," Vershinin said.

"You are aware, Sir, that dueling is forbidden," Uri said.

"Nevertheless, the challenge stands."

"What, no gauntlet thrown down to mark the occasion?" Roman said.

"Since you insist." Vershinin removed his white glove and slapped it hard across Roman's cheek. Roman's brow furrowed, and his hands clenched. He lunged forward. Uri and Fëdor grabbed him.

"Sunrise, Moskva River near the stone bridge." Vershinin stormed away.

Kira wiggled free from her mother's grasp and rushed to Roman. "This is not what I wanted. There is still time to end this foolishness if you apologize."

He stroked her cheek. "I do this not only for my honor but for yours." He looked over at her father.

Alexander led his daughter away. She turned her head back to Roman. "God be with you."

Boris leaned over to Roman. "Are you aware that

the Colonel is an infamous duelist? He has fought well over 100 without a severe injury."

"This time fate will turn against him," Roman said.

TEN

A GRAY MIST blanketed the landscape as dawn broke. The only sounds heard were the river lapping against the shoreline and an occasional frog's croak. Lanterns, dimly visible, crept toward each other in the gloom.

The tension was visible as four men met in silence—Roman, Uri, Vershinin, and Vershinin's second. Kira and the Countess stood nearby, along with Boris and Fëdor. They had summoned a doctor as added insurance. Sunlight flickered above the horizon as songbirds began their morning ritual, a stark contrast to the impending confrontation.

Vershinin's second spoke to Roman. "It is within the rules if you wish to announce your sincere apology for your offense and dispense with the duel."

"That in itself is an offense," Roman said.

Vershinin grunted with a toothy grin.

The Second opened a wooden chest. Roman and Uri inspected the green velvet-lined box that held two pistols and ramrods. The pistol handles were crafted from dark walnut. The lock plate and butt of the gun were of polished brass. Roman identified the set as seventeenth-century French.

"There will be no deloping or firing in the air." The Second said. "If neither man is hit, there will be another challenge until one is wounded or killed.

Kira gasped.

Vershinin gave her a disparaging look.

The Second continued. "I have a stash of lead balls."

Vershinin piped up. "We will set our pace at eight."

Roman knew the shorter the steps, the graver the insult. He thought Vershinin slurred his words and staggered a bit. *This may present an advantage.*

As Roman's Second and witness, Uri checked each pistol and made his selection. "I wish you would have asked Boris to stand in for you. He is better at this."

"Maybe, but I trust you more with my life," Roman said.

Uri half-cocked the jaw, pushed the frizzen forward, loaded the flint into the flash pan, and poured a sufficient amount of black powder down the barrel. He wrapped the lead ball in a cloth patch and dropped it down the muzzle. Taking the ramrod, he tamped down the powder and ball, primed the flash pan with a small amount of finely ground powder, fully cocked the pistol, and handed it to Roman.

"Careful, it may have a hair-trigger."

Roman and Vershinin stood back-to-back with loaded weapons in hand. Vershinin's Second counted the steps. "One—two—three …"

Roman wasn't used to the extra weight of a dueling pistol. Apprehension crept into his thoughts. *Focus, turn, and fire.*

"… seven—eight." Both men faced each other, presented their guns, and fired.

The songbirds went silent. Smoke curled up from the guns. Kira had not heard the explosion of the bullets as they left the barrels. She watched Roman's body jerk, his blood splatter before he crumbled to the ground. She rushed to his side. He lay unconscious on the cold ground. "You've killed him," she yelled and fell to her knees.

Vershinin, unscathed from the duel, gave her a hawkish stare and snarled. "We can only hope."

"I'll never forgive you," Kira said.

Vershinin stomped away.

Kira felt tears run down her cheeks and along the curves of her nostril as it touched her upper lip. She wiped them away with the back of her hand. "Where's the doctor?"

"He's right here." The Countess lifted her niece from the ground.

The doctor tore open Roman's blood-soaked shirt

while Kira held her breath. "It appears the bullet may have penetrated his left upper lung—barely missing the clavicle."

Kira exhaled. "Will he live?"

"I'll know more once we get him to the infirmary." The doctor motioned for Uri, Boris, and Fëdor to help move Roman into the carriage.

Kira clutched her hands to her cheeks. "Oh, Masha, what will I do if he dies?"

The Countess stroked her niece's back. "The doctor is the finest surgeon in Moscow."

THE DINGY INFIRMARY waiting room, with its cold linoleum floor and odor of disinfectant, made Kira think of death. The Countess sat beside her niece. Boris leaned against the wall. Fëdor chewed on his mustache. The room remained silent except for the click-clack of Uri's heels as he paced the floor.

Hours later, the doctor entered the waiting room in his bloodstained surgical gown. "We removed the bullet. He's lost a lot of blood but I'm optimistic about his recovery." A shout of hoorah from the fellows ignited everyone. "Be aware," the doctor frowned. "He is certain to suffer from shortness of breath all his life."

"It's my fault." Kira buried her face in her aunt's chest. The Countess wrapped her arms around her. "He is alive. Keep that in mind."

"May I see him?" Kira said.

"He is sleeping but you can visit for a few minutes.

Try not to wake him, dear."

Kira stood by Roman's bed, she felt her throat close up but suppressed the urge to cry, instead put on a brave front. *He looks so frail and helpless, like a precious little boy.*

Roman slowly opened his eyes. Their lustrous hazel coloring had taken on a gray hue. His lips parted, but no sound emitted.

"Hush, my love," Kira said. "I'm here with you."

The nurse came in and tried to usher Kira out of the room. "I can't leave him," she pleaded.

"Come dear, the patient needs his rest."

"I DON'T BELIEVE it." Alexander's ruddy complexion flushed redder than usual. He waved the paper in the air. "This report comes from sources who oppose my daughter's betrothal to Colonel Vershinin."

"I can assure you, Alexander," the Countess said. "I've had my people investigate him. The Tsar has funded Vershinin's gambling debt for years. He is penniless, in need of a fortune. He will certainly go through Kira's dowry … and then what will happen to her?"

"Oh sister, what will people say?" Kira's mother paced around the room.

Kira interrupted. "They will say I was fortunate to have escaped a dreadful fate."

Alexander strummed his fingers on the arm of the chair. Kira sat across from him, her thoughts reverting to Roman's recovery. She had visited him in the infirmary a few times a day during the past week. She fretted about him leaving for home soon after his discharge.

Alexander cleared his throat. "She will have to manage."

"Papa." Kira sat forward. "You can't mean to carry on with this charade?"

"He is a Romanov. What can we do?" Alexander remained steadfast while his wife wept in the background.

"You can threaten to cut off my dowry," Kira said. "If it is fortune he wants, he will not gain anything from me."

"Impractical," Alexander responded. "Gossip has reached the court. The scandal is on us."

Kira's mother exploded with a blaring wail.

"Woman—silence," he shouted.

"You can go to the Tsar and ask for special consideration," the Countess said.

"Impossible."

"You must implore the Colonel, Papa. Tell him the truth. I love another."

Alexander raised one eyebrow and said, "That he already knows."

Kira's mother continued to snivel.

"I had hoped to avoid telling you this with Kira present, but feel I have no choice," the Countess said. "My spies have communicated to me that Vershinin has cavorted for years in brothels and contracted the 'great pox.'"

There was a gasp from all.

"Kira will certainly succumb to blindness and insanity. Is this the life you wish for your daughter?"

Alexander rose from his seat. He pulled his fingers through what remained of his hair and buried his face in his hands. The women sat at the edge of their seats.

Alexander cleared his throat. "I shall speak to Mikhail Vershinin."

"We will be the gossip of Moscow and St. Petersburg. We will never be accepted at court. We will …" Her mother twisted her fingers and wept.

"Woman, what would you have me do? Subject our daughter to an abhorrent fate?" He stomped his foot. "Enough—it is done."

Kira hugged her father and kissed both his cheeks. "Thank you. Thank you. Thank you."

"Daughter, there are no assurances. The dissolution must come from the Colonel."

ELEVEN

ALEXANDER LOOMED OVER his daughter, his glare locked onto her with a furrowed brow. He exhaled with a grunt and plopped onto the yellow upholstered wingback chair.

Kira sat at attention and swallowed an acetic lump in her throat. She longed to push her father into revealing the hearsay but knew enough to remain quiet. She twisted and rubbed her hands until they turned red.

Kira's mother interjected, "Alexander, what did Colonel Vershinin say?"

"He consented to dissolve the marriage agreement."

Kira clapped once, then put her hands to her side. But she could not hide a broad grin.

Alexander furrowed his brow and continued, "Under conditions."

Kira sat upright. "Such as?"

He rose from his seat and raised a finger. "First, I am to provide him with a monthly allowance. It seems we will now be supporting his gambling." A mumble came from his wife. He held up his hand to quell them and paced. "Second, Kira is not allowed to attend any social events where he might be present."

"That suits me very well," Kira interrupted.

"We've lost our court connections," her mother moaned. "What will become of our other daughters?"

Her father's gaze turned stern. "Lastly, under no condition are you allowed to marry the Lieutenant."

"What?" Kira bristled.

Her mother pulled at Kira's dress to silence her, then spoke, "Alexander, I think you could approach the Tsar to find an honorable man with wealth and status for our daughter."

Kira sprang to her feet, her voice trembling with defiance. "I refuse to marry anyone except Roman Pavlovitch."

"Daughter, you will do as you are told." Alexander snapped.

Kira slumped back in her chair. Her lower lip protruded like that of a petulant three-year-old.

"Between Tsar Nicholas's beloved railroad project and the upcoming international peace conference, he has no time to waste on such inconsequential matters. Besides, now that the tittle-tattle is out, no one of prominence would consider her suitable for marriage."

Kira's mother started to whimper. "Maybe we can

look toward France or God forbid, England."

"I will elope," Kira declared.

"If you dare to continue in that manner you will be cut off from your dowry," her mother scolded.

"I don't care."

"You can't possibly think you can live without money and its finery after having it all your life."

"I can't possibly imagine my life without him," Kira replied.

"Ladies please, we won't resolve anything with this bickering. And, I don't want to lose my strong-minded daughter to an elopement. I've found out that the Lieutenant is being groomed for a high-ranking military career." Alexander sighed, "He may be our only hope. After all, he did save my life."

"What of Virshinin's condition?" her mother said.

"It is my opinion the Colonel is more afraid of the court gossip regarding his health than holding us accountable to an annulled engagement."

At that moment, Kira knew her father had consented to her marrying Roman. Her body radiated warmth and joy that she had never experienced before. She admired her father greatly for his political skill.

KIRA CRINGED AT the sounds of moans, coughs, and wheezes that filled the eight-bed ward. At the end of the room, an attendant mopped the floor with a pungent solution that stung the inside of Kira's nose. Her maid waited a distance away while Kira sat beside Roman's bedside.

"With all these sick people, it's a wonder anyone can regain one's health," Kira said. "I'm glad you'll be discharged tomorrow."

Pillows propped up, Roman rested his head against the wall and exhaled. "Yes."

"How is your wound?"

Roman tried to rotate his shoulder and winced. He massaged the incision at his upper left breast. "The doctor said the muscle will be stiff for a while." He caught his breath. "But if I continue to move it, I should regain full use. He said it was pure luck the bullet didn't shatter anything."

"The Lord be praised," Kira said and crossed herself.

"Amen," Roman replied.

"Where are Fëdor and Boris? I haven't seen them in days."

"Called back to St. Petersburg." He frowned. "I, too, must return."

Kira slouched her shoulders. "I have been trying to decide the right time to share something with you." She blushed, hesitated, and then said, "After the incident ..." She scanned the room to see if anyone was listening, then lowered her voice. "Boris told me about Colonel Vershinin's financial situation. You know." Roman nodded. "Auntie Masha, who was also present, decided to look further into his affairs. She reported to my father some rather disturbing health issues." Kira bit her lower lip, too horrified to say the word syphilis. "Papa had a long discussion with Vershinin. The engagement is off." Kira's voice carried a profound sense of relief as she shared the news, a smile that lifted her cheeks.

Roman sat upright in bed. A twinge of relief ran through his body. "What about your father? Won't this weaken his ties with the Tsar?"

"Not at all, Vershinin agreed to dissolve on good terms." She withheld the truth about the conditions Vershinin had placed on her and her family.

Roman took Kira's hands, raised them to his lips, and kissed one then the other. "I must speak to your father without delay."

ROMAN FELT HIS breakfast rise to his throat as the servant escorted him into the parlor. Alexander rested on a chaise and cast a severe expression his way. Roman swallowed hard, causing a sharp pain along his scar. "Sir." He clicked his heels, bowed, then returned to attention. His arm lay in a sling to prevent the stitches from splitting.

Alexander rose. "Let us step outside."

The lush tree-lined park with its rolling green hills stretched to the horizon. The warmth of the sun and fragrant fall blooms helped calm Roman's nerves, although he stuttered. "I … I." He paused, took a breath, and began again. "Sir, I've come to ask your permission for Kira's hand in marriage."

Alexander stopped walking and examined Roman.

"I don't hold great wealth," Roman said, "but my military career will provide a comfortable life. My promotion to captain is certain. I will command a company and follow a family tradition of rising in rank."

Alexander rubbed his chin. "My wife is not convinced you're a good match for our daughter."

Roman's shoulders collapsed. Kira had assured him that his offer was all but inevitable. He straightened his backbone. "My life is an empty vessel without Kira. I promise you that she will have a good life and never see a day of sorrow."

"My daughter is a high-spirited young woman. I had hoped to find a mature man who could tame that spirit … settle her down to find her rightful place in society."

"Sir, with all due respect, the one thing that makes Kira most endearing is her spirit."

Alexander shook his head. "I am not certain that constitutes a good marriage. You may find that quality unacceptable later. The things that most draw you to a person can later repel you."

Roman wondered if Alexander referred to his marriage.

"I believe you to be a good and honorable man," Alexander said. "After all, I owe you my life, and my daughter's." He paused, looked up to the heavens, then at Roman, and continued, "I am reluctant, but I give you my permission. But, I will hold you to your promise."

Roman, without thought, vigorously shook Alexander's hand. A sharp pain extended over his injury but did not supersede his joy.

TWELVE

The coldest days of winter were on their way out as the hint of early spring flowers peeped their heads above ground. It had been months since the duel, and social gossip had quelled most wagging tongues in St. Petersburg and Moscow.

Returning to St. Petersburg, Roman was eager to receive his promotion. The presence of Tsar Nicholas II and high-ranking generals at his commission added to the excitement. With his rise in rank came an increase in wages, and he had an eye on a little house in the countryside for Kira and himself. A sense of satisfaction reigned over his dominion. He was at a turning point in his life—things were finally falling into place.

Roman trotted Ivan past his company of stalwart soldiers standing at attention. The captain's bars across his shoulders weighed as heavily as his new responsibilities. Roman had regained most of his strength through rigorous military exercise. However, he still suffered from a lack of breath now and then. He finished his inspection and dismissed the unit. Uri pulled his horse alongside as they headed for the stables.

"Captain Pavlovitch." Uri enunciated Roman's promotion with a salute and a smile. "Congratulations. I want to again thank you for asking me to stand beside you at the altar."

"If not you—then who?" Roman winked.

"I hope the political upheaval we may soon confront stabilizes long enough to give you and Kira time to adjust to married life."

"Angry Japanese voices carry across Siberia. I fear another war is imminent," Roman said.

Uri said, "I heard Kolchak returned from the Arctic long enough to whisk his fiancé off to Siberia for a quick wedding before heading to Port Arthur."

"If nothing else, Kolchak is a fierce man of action." They laughed and dismounted.

"Roman, I would never say anything in front of Boris, but I hear the people don't have faith in their hearts for the Tsar."

"The newly formed labor party in Minsk may be cause for concern. The Tsar will hopefully provide them the opportunity to express their desires and demands or there could be a possibility of a revolution.

Even Tolstoy pleads that he consider a parliamentary government."

"I understand the Tsar went to Paris and studied the French parliament, but his consulates convinced him it would be unsound for Russia."

"The Kremlin has too many voices whispering in the Tsar's ear. These are turbulent times, my friend."

"OH, MOTHER, I need you to be happy for me," Kira said.

"At your father's insists, I relented now that your fiancé …" she cried into her handkerchief, "has been promoted." She dabbed her eyes and blew her nose. "It seems your man is in good standing with the Tsar, something about his grandfather saving the Tsar's grandfather. I don't understand. It's all too much for me."

"You see, everything is set to right." Kira twirled, emblematic of a ballerina. "I am getting married next month. Oh, Mama, I am so happy. Everything is too wonderful." She ran over to her mother and grasped both of her hands. "I want you to be as happy as I am."

"But what do we know about his family?"

"His father was killed at the battle of Shipka Pass at the end of the Russo-Turkish war, and his mother died of consumption in '94."

"Has he no brother … no sisters … no family?"

"Well." Kira wrung her hands. "He has a younger brother."

"Is he attending the wedding?"

"He can't."

Kira's mother tilted her head to one side and raised an eyebrow.

"Now Mother, don't get upset." Her voice was low and cautious. "He was sent to Siberia as a conspirator in an uprising."

Kira's mother flung her arms in the air. "God be with us. What will people say?"

"No one needs to know. It will be our secret."

"Until it's not." She turned to her daughter. "Does your father know?"

"He has some concerns but keep in mind Roman is in good standings with the Tsar."

"For now. But what about your future."

"Mother, please, please, please be happy for me."

"I am trying … but it's just too much."

The bedroom door opened, and the Countess entered, followed by a servant carrying a bulky package. "Oh, Auntie," Kira rushed to her side. "Please talk to Mama. She needs to fill her heart with love."

"Sister, this is a time for celebration not tears," Countess said. "Kira, I have brought you something." She presented Kira with the package.

Kira untied the red satin ribbon, lifted the box lid, and unfolded the tissue. "Oh, Masha." Kira stood stunned for a moment. She pulled out a full-length brown silver cast sable coat. "Mama, look at what

Auntie has given me. Only the noblest wear such fur."

"Sister, it's too generous."

The Countess dismissed her sister's envious tone. "You can add it to your trousseau."

"Mother gave me her favorite sideboard. I have linen and bedding." Her cheeks turned a rosy hue. "Roman has found us a lovely cottage in the country. We will be so happy." Kira waltzed around with her fur.

"We must celebrate." The Countess addressed her servant. "Bring us vodka ... no, let's have French champagne."

ROMAN RETURNED TO Moscow to follow the age-old Russian tradition of paying a ransom for his bride as a token of his love and commitment. He arrived at Kira's home, where her father presented the bride, shrouded in a long opaque veil.

"Sir, I ask permission for your daughter's hand in marriage."

Alexander said, "The family demands a dowry of riches."

"Sir, I haven't great wealth, but I can offer you the most precious thing I have—my horse."

A gasp rang out from the other room. Roman's eyes widened, he turned his head to the sound.

Alexander rubbed his chin. "Agree." They shook hands and Alexander handed over his daughter.

In anticipation, Roman lifted the veil to reveal

Kira but was shocked to see a young girl—Kira's youngest sister.

Laughter exploded from the other room as Kira, her mother, and sisters entered. Even Alexander had a good belly laugh. Roman was relieved it was all in fun, and he did not need to hand over his beloved, Ivan.

Kira's parents arranged a formal celebration to introduce Roman into their exclusive social group. The drawing room rugs were rolled up to provide a dance floor and bouquets of fragrant flowers provided a sweet aroma. The sunny day allowed the terrace doors to be open so the guests could spill out onto the veranda. Even Kira's grandmother, Baba, attended.

Kira's mother had laid out her finest china. She arranged to have blini stations with jams, fruits, and diminutive sandwiches. The finest black and green teas were poured from hand-painted, lavishly gilded blue and white porcelain samovars. Not to be outdone by delicious candies and tea cakes.

Kira placed her hand on Roman's arm as he led her to the dance floor. They brushed passed a cluster of women to overhear their conversation.

"Seems all that German can do is produce girls. Where is the boy to become the next Tsar?"

"She has brought misfortune to our homeland."

The women's voices were filled with disdain.

"The Tsar does not have the iron will of his father."

"I fear for the loss of this great nation."

They stopped talking when one motioned to the others that Roman was within earshot. He did not disagree with their opinions; on the contrary, his concern was the amount of division that might have spread throughout the country. But their words vanished from his mind like a shooting star at the sight of Kira's radiance. He was spellbound with anticipation regarding their future together.

THIRTEEN

1900

ROMAN STOOD IN a secluded area away from the nave of the wedding chapel with Uri, his groomsman, by his side. Both men wore full-dress uniforms of dark trousers and red tunic tops. An array of medals flashed across their chests. Roman tugged on his tunic and fiddled with his cap.

Uri said, "I can hear your knees knocking and your face has lost all color."

"I think running full speed into battle is less nerve-racking. I could use a shot of vodka."

"You consumed enough last night. You should still be drunk."

"My nerves wore that off long ago. God, I wish this were over."

"Soon, brother, soon." Uri passed a flask of vodka and patted Roman on the back.

KIRA'S MOTHER SAT next to her daughter and rubbed her back. "Kira …" She paused for a long moment, her voice gentle. "Your purpose as a woman is here. You will give yourself to your husband tonight. This is part of marriage. It is natural, not to be confusing or fearful." She put her handkerchief to her mouth.

"Mother, it will be all right. Roman is a kind and gentle man—not a beast. I am not afraid."

"I just … I want you to be happy in your new life." She pulled Kira's hair away from her shoulder and smoothed it down her back.

Kira kissed her mother on the cheek. "I will. Our love for each other is stronger than Saint Basil. Nothing will ever tear us apart."

THE WEDDING PROCESSION took place at the Countess's church in Moscow. Inside, a plethora of flickering candles emitted a sweet aroma that provided a romantic ambiance. There was little space between guests in the seventy-seat chapel. The organist started, and the crowd hushed.

The Russian Orthodox ceremony commenced with the reading of scriptures, followed by a sermon and the sacrament of wine and bread. A gray-bearded priest in a gold robe placed the wedding rings on the Holy Table, which was covered with plain linen, symbolizing the cloth that wrapped Christ in his tomb.

The priest blessed the rings. "Bless, O Lord, these rings and grant that he who gives and she who shall wear it remain faithful to each other and abide in peace and live together in love until their lives end. Through Jesus Christ our Lord. Amen."

Roman and Kira stood inside the church entrance. She wore an eggshell-colored, heavily embroidered lace gown. The bodice cinched tight at the waist, flattered her figure. Behind her stretched an elaborate ten-foot train. Atop her head lay a petite diamond tiara attached to a sheer veil.

The priest traced the sign of the cross above their heads with a blessing. He presented each of them with a lit candle and said a brief prayer for the couple before blessing the rings again. He slid the rings onto each couple's right hand, a gesture of unity. Then led them down the aisle into the center of the church, where they stepped on a piece of rose-colored fabric, symbolizing their entry into a new life. Kira and Roman professed they were marrying of their own free will and had not promised themselves to another. After the priest's prayer, Kira's eldest sister held the crown over Kira's head, and Uri held a crown over Roman. Their vows were exchanged, and a common cup of wine was shared. Roman took the opportunity to indulge in a generous sip. At the same time, Kira shifted in her tight shoes, with thoughts of slipping out of them.

The priest joined their hands and wrapped them in a red sash. Roman felt the heat from Kira's palm. Their eyes locked, and Roman squeezed her hand. Her gaze calmed his nerves, and he relaxed his shoulders. After a final sign of the cross and blessing, the priest presented the couple to the audience. Roman leaned over to Kira and said, "My love is eternal, Kira Pavlovitch."

"Till death, us do part, my love," she said.

THE RECEPTION CONVENED in a mesmerizing hall of mirrors at Masha's estate. Kira and Roman sat at the heart of a 50-foot table amidst cobalt and gold-rimmed china that rested on a blue and white laced tablecloth. Delicate flowers were set in low vases to ensure guests could clearly see each other. Burning candelabras reflected a warm glow enhanced by the mirrors. Soothing notes from chamber music flowed in from an adjoining room.

Alexander rose from his seat and clinked his glass to quiet the guests. "It seems only yesterday when I held my daughter in my arms for the first time." His voice was thick with emotion. "And now … here you are … a grown woman heading off to start a new life." He raised his glass. "To the health of the newlyweds. May your days together be forever, *Na zdorovye.*"

The guests shouted, "Groko, groko, groko." A servant poured a shot of groko, a bitter alcohol made from horseradish root, into each glass. Kira grimaced before she downed the shot. The couple kissed as the guests counted the seconds, "One, two, three, four, five …" Kira heard the encouragement from the quests and tried not to giggle. When their lips parted, Roman gently kissed her a second time, whereupon they raised their glasses in a toast.

Roman stood and addressed the guests. "Kira and I wish to thank you all for joining us on this happiest of occasions. The moment I laid eyes on this stunning vision at the Summer Palace, I knew we were destined to be together. To my beautiful bride." The room erupted in applause as the couple shared a loving kiss.

Uri, Boris, and Fëdor bounced up in unison. "Kira, we love you, but I hope you know what you've gotten yourself into." Laughter exploded, and everyone broke into song.

The joyous atmosphere was interrupted by the arrival of a heavyset man staggering into the room. The guests grew quiet, and the music stopped. Alexander rose from his chair. Voices murmured, "What is he doing here?"

Alexander started to approach. "Colonel Mikhail Vershinin."

Before Alexander could say another word, Vershinin raised his arm, almost losing his balance. "I have a gift for the newlyweds." He pulled a silver flask from inside his breast pocket. Instead of giving them the flask, he opened it and gulped a swig. "To the bride." He paused to regain his balance and then took another swig. The flask slipped from his fingers and crashed to the floor with a pang, and he followed with a thud. Alexander snapped his fingers, and servants hurriedly gathered the drunk, the flask, and escorted him away.

The music started again. A servant set a round bread loaf decorated with pastry images of flowers, leaves, and ears of wheat that lay on an embroidered towel in front of the couple. Along with the bread was a wheel of cheese. Every guest was presented with a sample of each. The feast also included a rich tapestry of various poultries, meats, and an abundance of alcohol.

As the sun began to rise, the guests made their way into the music hall. Roman took Kira's hand and led her to the dance floor. Kira had chosen the Strauss waltz that had played at their first meeting.

Roman said, "Are you ready Mrs. Pavlovitch?"

"I like the sound of that."

"I like saying it."

They danced one more dance and then made their way up the stairs to the bridal chamber while the merriment continued.

FOURTEEN

SUMMER ROLLED INTO fall late that year. Kira's sunny disposition blew in with a chill that turned sour. Roman tried to comfort her with compliments on her appearance, cooking, and needlework. Nothing seemed to sway her mood.

"Why don't you go into the city tomorrow and visit friends?"

"Everyone I know has gone back to Minsk or Moscow. There is no one to visit."

Days rolled on, but Kira's restlessness was a constant companion. Roman wrote Masha out of concern and asked her to visit them at their country cottage.

MASHA'S ARRIVAL BRIGHTENED Kira's mood for a time. "Kira, my dear, I have been here for several days, and you seem distracted, confused, and out of sorts. What's the matter?"

"Oh Masha, It's been only a few months since we married and I do feel guilty for not being enthralled about my new life with Roman, but … I miss all the excitement. The planning, the parties, the ceremony. I'm so isolated in this little house in the country without family and friends. I feel all the joy has drained from my soul."

"Have you spoken to Roman about this?"

"I'm afraid he will think I'm an ungrateful beast."

"I have never seen two people more in love with each other. You will overcome this moment and move forward. Maybe you both could take a vacation. Or you might travel to Minsk to visit your mother."

"I can't run home to mother. How might that look?" Kira bit her lower lip. "The worst of it is that I … I … I don't have a baby." She cried into her hands. "I should have a baby growing in me by now."

Masha patted Kira's shoulder. "My dear, this can take time, and with your frayed nerves, well, you need to relax. It will happen for you." She paused. "I will get tickets to the Mariinsky Theatre. We can all go out for dinner and then enjoy the ballet."

"How wonderful." Kira threw her arms around her aunt.

THEY RODE THE train into the city and hired a coach to the restaurant. Roman held his bride's hand. Kira, still troubled, felt comforted by her husband as they bounced along the rutted road. Masha sat opposite, next to her widower friend. They exchanged polite conversation to ease the tension.

The coach stopped suddenly. Kira pulled back the curtain and peered out at the gas-lit streets. A gaunt face of a child with hollow-haunted eyes stared back. Bony legs poke out below short-ragged pants. Fingers extended, looking for a handout. Kira quickly closed the curtain.

"Disturbing isn't it?" The widower said.

Kira pretended not to hear. The coach continued.

"Living conditions are unsanitary and crowded. In some cases, as many as five people rotate their time in a single cot while the other works for enough food to eat," the widower said.

"The Tsar chooses to ignore his people's plight," Roman said.

"This Tsar is not the power his father was."

With a worried eye, Kira clenched her jaw and squeezed Roman's arm.

"This is why I live in Moscow far from the politics of Petersburg," Masha said.

"My Dear," the widower said. "Muscovites are suffering too."

"Enough of this morose talk," Kira said. "We are almost at the Palkin restaurant."

After Kira and Roman exited the coach, Kira drew Roman aside. "Please don't talk about politics tonight. I'd hate to have you overheard."

"Thank you for your concern, but I know when to hold my tongue."

Captivating pipe organ music vibrated as they entered the establishment. Inside, a large room boasted an elaborately designed 20-foot high ceiling, curved crown molding, and a less-than-fancy setting of simple tables arranged around the room. A stark contrast to the opulence above. The maître d' rushed up to Masha and bowed. "Countess Sheremeteva, welcome. It is good to see you again."

"We are happy to be here tonight," she said.

He escorted them to a quiet corner table. They strolled past a fish tank with live sturgeon. "Those are the ugliest fish I have ever seen," Kira said.

"Yes, but what they provide is heavenly," Masha said.

Without ordering, champagne was delivered, followed by caviar with a side of petite pancakes and *crème fraîche*.

"Umm, this black jam is quite tasty," Kira said.

Masha smiled at her niece.

Later, they consumed courses of consommé, fish cakes, game, beefsteak, and crepe Suzette for dessert.

At the ballet, Kira heard Masha's friend snoring. She elbowed Roman as his head began to sink into his chest. The ride home was quiet, with everyone in their thoughts. Kira enjoyed the evening but was concerned about the earlier conversation about Roman's disdain regarding the Tsar.

AS FALL HAD arrived late, winter, on the other hand, came early. Roman sent Kira to Moscow to visit her aunt before they prepared to accompany the Romanov family to Crimea. They corresponded daily by letter.

> My Love,
> Masha has been so absolutely wonderful. We attended the Bolshoi ballet, where they performed Swan Lake. It was extraordinarily marvelous. I wish you had been here to enjoy it with me. I am burning for a kiss and long to be tight in your arms. I Love you with all my heart. God bless you, my darling.
> Yours forever,
>
> Kira.

> My Beloved,
> Thank you for your delightful letters and wishes. Missing you terribly. I am kissing you tenderly.
> R

Roman felt the bond between them tighten even with the distance. But as the days rolled on, waiting to depart for Crimea, the echo of his footsteps along the wooden floor grew louder, a haunting reminder of his solitude. His mind twisted and turned, and the only sound he heard was his heartbeat. His loneliness for Kira prompted him to room with the musketeers. Uri, Boris, and Fëdor were happy to have Roman back in the fold.

"Since you got married, we hardly see you," Uri said, "except during drills or while passing in the halls."

"It's been difficult splitting my time between my responsibilities and my relationships. I've spent the last 10 years living with the men in this company. It's strangely different living with a woman." He combed his finger through his hair. "They are so messy. Clothes everywhere, money being spent that I don't have, and the worst … the mood changes. One minute she is up, the next crying in the bedroom. But I wouldn't change a thing to have her at my side this instant."

Uri laughed. "You will be fine. Give it time for both of you to settle into a pattern. Once you have a child, things will take a turn."

"A child." He raised his voice. "I can't begin to think about what that addition might bring."

Uri laughed. "Okay, boys where are we off to tonight?"

FIFTEEN

ROMAN DEPARTED THE train at the Moscow station. His heart raced in anticipation of seeing his wife as he hurried to hail a coach. He shaded his eyes from the bright, warm sun yet noticed the damp streets. The air was crisp and pleasant, a stark contrast to the typical smoke-hazed, pungent city stench.

The coachman warned Roman that he needed to take side streets to avoid angry crowds voicing their discontent with living and working conditions. Roman nodded and climbed inside. He had experienced the same issues in the capital when a mob tried to gain entrance to the Winter Palace. Little did they know that since the uprisings started, the Tsar and his family resided at Tsarskoe Selo, outside the capital.

Roman arrived at the Countess' home to collect Kira for their trip to Crimea. He received a heart-warming sight when Kira swung open the front door.

Before he stepped onto the landing. She raced into his arms and held tight.

"I missed you, my love."

Roman responded with a long kiss.

"Come inside you two before neighbors' tongues start to waggle," the Countess said. "I have tea and cakes set up in the drawing room."

Kira sat close to Roman and braced her body next to his. The Countess served everyone. "How was your trip?"

"Uneventful, thankfully."

"With all the strife the train timetables are unreliable these days."

Kira scrunched her nose at the politics being discussed and changed the topic. "Masha is going to treat us to an evening out before we begin our summer holiday," Kira said.

"Keep in mind, I am on duty there," Roman said.

"I believe the Tsarina will enlist wives to assist her in sewing garments for the poor," Masha said.

"That will be grand." Kira sipped her tea.

THEY ARRIVED IN Sevastopol in time to witness the Navy's ceremonial welcome for the Tsar. The royal family would spend a few days sailing around the Black Sea to Yalta on their yacht. Roman and Kira looked forward to relaxing in town and doing some local sightseeing before heading to Livadiya.

Kira inhaled the refreshing salt air. "It's sort of a

fishy, tangy smell. I've never experienced anything like it before." She pointed to the porcelain-white lime-stone homes nestled along the tree-lined cliffs and admired the picturesque scene. "It's a lovely hamlet. I could stay here forever."

"Don't get used to it, my darling. We eventually have to return to the capital."

They retired to a room in a villa outside of town that Roman had arranged. French doors opened onto a veranda that faced the sea. In the foreground, hedgerows crisscrossed the hillside. Kira closed her eyes and lifted her face to the sun. Roman approached her from behind, embraced her, turned her around, and gently kissed her.

After a hearty breakfast, they set out to visit a monastery. High above them lay the ivory tower surrounded by a long retaining wall carved out of a cliff. They trekked up the steep staircase.

Kira reached the top and bent over. "I can't believe how breathless and light-headed I am."

Roman grabbed her arm to steady her. "Let's head back to the hotel."

"No. I'll be all right in a moment. Also, you want to visit the crypt at St. Vladimir's Cathedral and say a prayer at your late uncle's tomb."

"Mother might never forgive me or would at the least haunt me if I don't pay homage to those who lost their lives during the Crimean War."

They returned to their carriage and drove around the cape to enjoy the warm day and seaside views.

"I'll be sad to leave this place, but I look forward to seeing Livadiya tomorrow," Kira said.

LIVADIYA WAS A countryside of unbroken pine-forested mountains. The valley floor flourished with pink and white blossoms of apples, cherries, peaches, and almonds wafting in a perfumed garden that stretched to a sapphire sea. The Greek revival-style Summer Palace resided in the distance, among a sprawling landscape.

"Oh Roman, we are so lucky to be amidst such beauty. I hear the marble floors were imported from Italy and they have an Arabic garden."

Roman smiled at his bride.

KIRA SPENT THE summer swimming in the Black Sea, in a section designated 'for ladies only.' The women wore cotton bathing skirts that rested barely above the knee with a sailor-type top with puffy sleeves. Roman managed his regiment's duties of providing security for the Romanovs. Kira had declined invitations to play tennis and go horseback riding. Roman noticed her lack of energy, headaches, and light sensitivity. He insisted she seek medical help and made an appointment.

Days later, joyous news arrived that the mouse had died and Kira was with child. She was due early the following year. Roman was overjoyed with slight trepidation at the responsibility of becoming a father. He picked her up and spun her around, then suddenly froze. He carefully placed her on the chaise.

She giggled, "I won't break, silly."

Kira spent the remaining days of summer sewing and writing letters to her family. On one occasion, the Tsarina sent her an invitation to attend a sewing circle. Kira spent a good part of the morning deciding what to wear. She selected a khaki lightweight cotton skirt and lace blouse.

"How was your day at the palace?" Roman said.

"I didn't see much other than the parlor where we sat in a circle and sewed. The hovering attention of a holy man in the Tsarina's presence made an uncomfortable situation." She rubbed her belly. "I never realized how religious she was … crucifixes and icon paintings everywhere. Their cold, scrutinizing gaze followed my every move. The smell of incense and the sound of the holy man's deep, resonating voice added to the discomfort. It made my spine crawl.

"I feel sorry for them … prisoners of their heritage, trapped in a macabre, medieval ritual of protocol," Roman said.

"Yes, I don't envy them in the least," Kira said. "What shall we have for supper?"

By the end of summer, things were packed up for the

journey back to St. Petersburg. Roman and Kira were privileged to ride in the royal train. Roman believed it was because both she and the Tsarina were expecting. Although in a separate car, the accommodations were still stunning, with plush sofas and chairs.

A servant placed a tray of tea and cakes on the table and exited the room.

"It's unsettling surrounded by such opulence while beyond these windows, people are enduring hardships," Roman said.

Kira poured for everyone. "Yes my dear, but what are we to do about it?"

Roman fell back in his chair. "I'm thinking of transferring to a different unit."

She looked at Roman, which caused her to overfill her teacup. Liquid flowed onto the tray. She hurried to soak up the spill with a cloth napkin. "Please promise me you will wait until after the baby is born."

"Don't worry, nothing definite." He kissed her forehead and reached for his tea.

SIXTEEN

1901/1902

WINTER GENERATED EXCITEMENT for Kira. With the pending arrival of a newborn, the attention she had gained before the wedding was once again upon her. Tea parties were held in her honor. Roman remained anxious about the responsibility at home and beyond. The country's unrest, marked by the increased rhetoric from Trotsky, Lenin, and the Bolsheviks, was a constant backdrop to their lives, shaping their decisions and fears.

Despite the societal pressure for pregnant women to remain secluded, Kira refused to stay cloistered. Instead, she wore a maternity corset to disguise her belly and continued to shop and attend small gatherings, albeit to the dismay of some matrons. At one such gathering, she sat with an assembly of mothers who filled her head with strange advice.

"Don't think ugly thoughts or your baby will be deformed. Get plenty of fresh air, at least two hours a day. Drink champagne to relieve nausea and consume dark ale to keep up your strength. However, don't drink anything bitter or salty, or your child will have a sour disposition."

Kira listened and nodded, taking it in stride with some skepticism. Roman voiced concern when she relayed the conversation to him. Still, she reassured him that her mother had given her sound advice and had survived several births herself.

During the last few weeks of her pregnancy, Kira remained housebound. Constant commode runs, lack of sleep, and the baby's movement made it too difficult for her to venture far. However, she found joy in feeling the baby somersault and cartwheel after dinner. Not the typical father-to-be, Roman rubbed her belly and told the baby it would be courageous, honorable, and do noteworthy things.

Kira's mother arrived before the birth. Although she was there to assist her daughter, she continually complained about this or that not being right or questioned why things were done a certain way. To Kira's dismay, her mother rearranged the kitchen and drawing room. Roman found excuses to remain with his regiment until nightfall, returning in time to eat supper and retire.

ANYA MARIA PAVLOVITCH was born in early 1902 with a full head of auburn hair and healthy lungs. Kira had an exhaustive breech delivery. She apologized for the arrival of a daughter instead of a son. Roman dismissed her regret and anxiety, pleased to have a healthy child. "She will be ours and ours alone," he expressed.

For the most part, Anya's disposition was calm and easy-going, similar to sailing on smooth water, but on occasion, fits of temper could capsize the boat. At that moment, Mother stepped in to rescue her frazzled daughter.

"Kira," her mother rocked the baby to sleep, "has Roman told you when he will receive his new orders?"

Kira swallowed hard. "Mother, I shouldn't have said anything to you. It's vital that you keep that to yourself."

"Yes. Yes, Dear."

Kira wrung her hands with worry that her mother might blab to the village and cause harm to Roman's appointment.

While preparing the evening meal, her mother criticized how she prepared *Zharkoe*. Don't cook the potatoes too long and make sure the beef is cooked thoroughly. "Yes, Mother." Kira ignored her instructions and continued with her recipe, causing her mother to leave in a snit pretending to check on the baby.

Later that evening, everyone relaxed beside a

crackling fire. Kira heard continual sighs from her mother. "What's the matter?"

"Oh, nothing."

Kira glanced over at Roman, who raised his eyebrows and shrugged.

When she left the room, Roman leaned over and whispered. "When do you think your mother is going to return home?"

"I'm feeling stronger and more comfortable with the baby. I will suggest her family needs her."

A few days later, her mother departed, leaving Kira with a saddened heart. Although she appreciated her mother's help, she still felt a bit apprehensive on her own. On the other hand, Roman was happy it was finally the three of them.

DAYS TURNED INTO weeks and weeks into months. Anya was walking, although her stride was more of a lurch forward with a wide stance and outstretched arms—reminiscent of Frankenstein's monster. Once she gained stability, she raced around while Kira panted after her. Roman gave way to bouts of sullen behavior at the lack of Kira's attention. Kira doted on Anya, believing her focus was on raising a healthy and respectful daughter, not catering to her husband's every need.

Roman witnessed the disparity between social classes close up and the blatant refusal of the Tsar to assist his starving people. Factions within the working class grew angrier, yet things remained relatively calm. Since the creation of the Socialist Revolutionary Party two years prior, Roman felt an uprising was inevitable. He thought about his brother, Artie. Roman had not reflected on him in years. He had disowned Artie when he was exiled to Siberia for inflaming farmers to strike. His brother's conduct had made it awkward between Roman and the Tsar. Roman questioned whether the Tsar truly trusted him after Artie's incident. Torn between his loyalty, duty as an imperial guard, and his family's safety, Roman considered a way to reduce the possible strain.

War rumors with rival Japan circulated within the palace. The Tsar's advisors assured him that Japan was too weak and would never attack. However, the exculpating tension over the Korean peninsula, the naval base in Port Arthur, and a Russian stronghold in Manchuria caused Japan to feel under threat. There was also pressure from his third cousin Wilhelm urging him to hold the "Yellow Peril" and save Europe from Asian aggression.

Roman decided to seize the opportunity and request a transfer to the Far East.

SEVENTEEN

1903/1904

ROMAN PACED THE parlor floor with his hands clasped behind his back, reminiscent of an expectant father. Kira watched him pace while Anya wiggled on her lap. Kira's mind reeled about what worried her husband. He stopped and turned. She swallowed hard in anticipation of his thoughts.

"The Japanese have broken off negotiations with Russia." He sighed. "The Kaiser has named the Tsar as Emperor of the Pacific, he of course being Emperor of the Pacific. This could potentially lead to war with Japan." He returned to pacing. "I've been searching for an opportunity to transfer. Port Arthur is a way to escape the insanity here." His voice was as unsure as his beliefs.

Kira placed Anya on the floor and rose to her feet. "I fear war." Her voice trembled. "What if you don't come back, or worse you're taken prisoner, or God forbid killed." Her voice reached a high octave filled with anxiety. "You promised my father that I would never see a day of sorrow."

"I can't stand by as this incompetent government crumbles before my eyes. I need to be a part of something greater to ensure the survival of Russia."

"Your priority is here, protecting your family."

"Don't you see? Without a country, we lose security, civility, and principles. We lose everything we hold precious."

"There are thousands of soldiers. Why must you be among them?"

"Do you think I can easily forego duty and honor? My heritage is something that has been ingrained into my soul?"

Kira buried her face in her hands and began to sob. "I won't survive without you."

Roman wrapped his arms around his wife. "Not to worry. It's not my time to die."

Anya wrapped her arms around both parents' legs. Roman picked her up, and the three remained in a tight embrace.

URI SAT FORWARD in his seat. "What the hell, Roman. You're off to the Far East?"

"Why are you shocked at my new assignment? We've talked about the discord within the ranks. In my unit, there are disgruntled undertones and I've had a few defect to the socialists."

"God, don't let Boris hear about it or he'll have every man whipped until they confess, even if they aren't discontented."

They drank a shot of vodka and simultaneously fell back in their chairs.

"What about Fëdor?" Uri said. "Where do you think he stands?"

"He's Boris's puppet. Although, maybe not, but you never know where his loyalty reside at any one time." Roman paused. "I need you to watch over Kira. See that she has everything she needs for herself and Anya. I've tried to get her to go home or to her aunt's but she refuses."

Uri nodded.

They downed another shot.

"You heard that the Tsar finally has a son?" Uri said.

"Yes, after four daughters, he must be pleased."

"What about you? Do you wish for a son?"

"Kira had such a difficult time one seems be the right number."

They consumed more vodka with a toast to life.

"When do you leave?"

"By the end of the week. I will take the train to Moscow then change trains and continue over the Urals through Siberia and Manchuria."

"Will you stop and see your brother?"

"I've thought about it but I'm not certain where to find him."

"I may have a way. I'll check and get back to you."

IT WAS A grim, rainy day on which tears flowed. Uri, Fëdor, Kira, and Anya saw Roman off at the train station. Uri mentioned that Boris would not or could not find the time to see him off.

Families were loading onto the train, making their way home as summer ended. A sweet smell lingered in the air, bringing the promise of hope, Roman thought.

Uri said, "There will be a surprise waiting for you in Irkutsk."

Roman grasped Uri by the forearm. "Keep safe my brother."

"You too." Uri hugged Roman and slapped him on the back.

Fëdor chewed his mustache and kicked the ground with the toe of his boot.

"Fëdor, take care of yourself. Express to Boris, I wish him well," Roman said.

The train whistle pierced the air, a stark reminder of the impending departure. Roman leaped onboard as the engine jerked forward. He blew his family a kiss.

"Write as soon as you arrive." Kira clutched Anya to her hip. She waved Anya's hand. "Say goodbye to Papa."

KIRA RECEIVED HER first letter a month later.
    My Love,
        Missing you and Anya.
        Uri kept his promise and arranged for Artie

to meet me at the train station. It was a brief but heartfelt reunion. Artie is among the many forced laborers working on the rails. He is in good spirits despite his situation. Our visit was short, only long enough to wait for another train to pass in the opposite direction. I can't help but wonder when our paths will cross again, but I hope this is not the last time I see him.

Fortunately, I arrived in Port Arthur after three weeks of hard travel before winter took root. It's a picturesque setting and would be quite a lovely place to visit if not for the grim reality of what we face. The surrounding hills will shield the harbor from the effects of the freezing blasts of winter wind that barreled in from the Arctic, keeping the port ice-free all year round—ideal for the navy.

This town has two sections, old and new. The older section has narrow, unpaved streets with rundown warehouses and shabby residential buildings. The newer section had tree-lined avenues and modern buildings similar to what you'd see back home.

A stone fortress stands tall against the pigeon-gray skies at the top of one of the hills. My mission is to strengthen the port's defense. There are over 50,000 soldiers with an incredible array of modern equipment. We have commandeered hundreds of Chinese to dig trenches, making it easy for men, guns, and supplies to pass between each fortification. There is a shortage of barbed wire, but one of the men came up with using a telegraph line. It's ingenious. With such ingenuity, we are certain to win this war.

The distance from home weighs heavy on my heart, and I long to hear updates from you. Please write soon.

Yours faithfully,

R

Kira carefully folded the letter and pressed it into her favorite book, Anna Karenina. She picked up Anya, rocked her in her arms, and finger-combed her hair. "We shall see Papa soon."

IT WOULD BE months until Kira received another letter.

My Darling Kira,

I write to you with trepidation as the war is upon us and not going well. The Japanese launched a surprise attack before sunrise. Knowing the deteriorating relations, our Chief Admiral did nothing to protect the fleet. Our battleships are all but gone—torpedoed. I fear we no longer hold any power in the Pacific.

We are dug into the hillside for protection. Huge shells pass overhead that sound like a roaring train. Waves of Japanese infantry climb the steep hill. We mow them down, but they continue like a swarm of ants. The carnage is brutal and hard to witness, let alone describe. Bodies are severed in half from machine guns. The Japanese use their dead as fortification and continue to maneuver up the hill. The moans from the dying echo through-out the night.

I long to be home in your arms.

Men and supplies are low. The railway is still not completed, and with all the winter storms, there are mountainous delays in the availability of ammunition, weapons, food, and clothing. We were doomed before it started. France refuses to come to our aid—traitors. But worst of all, after pushing us into this war, the Kaiser turned his support to the Japanese. He is the evilest of men. I feel I'm in some kind of a dream, a surreal state of disorientation and disbelief, with the speed at which we have advanced to disaster.

I can only see this conflict lasting a bit longer. Hopefully, I will be home this time next year, God willing.

Love to you both,

R

My Darling Roman,

Good to receive your letter, my love. Things are not going well at home. I have witnessed starvation firsthand and now understand your fears. The underweight, gaunt-faced, and bloated stomachs of the children are shocking. It defies all humanity.

A bulletin from Port Arthur has set off protests against the Tsarist regime. Last Sunday, the Imperial Guard shot and killed unarmed demonstrators, women, and children as they tried to petition the Tsar at the Winter Place. I pray our friends were not a part of such brutality. The people who once thought of the Tsar as their champion now hold him personally responsible for the massacre. The news reported that socialists threw a bomb into the lap of a Grand Duke and blew him to bits. Other royals are being murdered. We are all afraid to venture from our homes.

The revolt has been crushed here in St. Petersburg and Moscow. Still, the peasants continue to burn barns and manor houses in the countryside. There is a rumor that the crew of a battleship rebelled against its officers and sought asylum in Romania. I fear for Russia.

I've had to release the housekeeper as things are not so good. Uri comes as often as possible to bring food and supplies to ensure our safety. He is such a dear. I don't know how we could survive without his kindness. You would be very proud of me, as I have learned to cook a scrumptious borscht.

I long to gaze into your eyes and hold you tight. Anya cries for her papa. Remain safe and come home soon.

All my love,
Kira

Although grateful to Uri, Kira had become concerned about his attention—almost devotion. It had been over a year since Kira watched Roman leave for the Far East. Uri appeared more often lately and with gifts—nesting dolls for Anya and the novel *The Brothers Karamazov* for herself. She avoided relaying her concerns to Roman, dismissing Uri's behavior due to her overactive imagination. Her thoughts solely remained on Roman's return.

EIGHTEEN

1904

THE AIR WAS filled with the stench of burnt gunpowder mixed with rotting corpses strewn across the landscape. Messages reported the dire news that the Russian Navy could no longer assist the ground troops. The port was flooded with Japanese ships, and the enemy had advanced from the northeast by land. Once they crossed the Yalu River, Port Arthur would be surrounded. Roman thought of Pushkin's poem "Napoleon." How a tyrant's thirst for war ended him imprisoned on an island. *After this inevitable defeat, what will be the Tsar's fate?*

General Stassen sent the enemy a message to offer their surrender. Roman believed it cowardice that drew the General to consider such a rash decision, given the vast store of food and ammunition. Word returned that the enemy had allowed the officers to leave on the promise that they would no longer engage in military action. Roman, fully aware of the consequences, disregarded the pledge, believing it void of merit.

> My Darling,
>
> This may be the last letter that finds you. We are in a crisis and trying to retreat before we are captured and taken prisoner. There is talk that the President of America is negotiating a peace treaty. I will make my way home, but it may be some time before I see you. Remain vigilant and keep yourself and the baby safe.
>
> Yours lovingly,
>
> R

Roman and a few other disgruntled officers heard of a raging battle at Mukden, a possible pivotal conflict, and headed north. They camped along the roadside and ate the food they had stuffed in their knapsacks. They ate their food cold to avoid lighting up the sky in case the enemy was near. Roman, still suffering shortness of breath from the injury he received during the duel, felt exhausted and ready for a night's rest. He hunkered down, wrapped in a long wool fur-lined coat and wool socks that kept him warm until dawn.

The four-day trek on foot had been a disappointment. By the time they arrived, the army was encircled and in disarray. The battle was lost. They met with General Samsonov, who was in retreat and grumbling about General Rennenkampf's Cossack division.

Roman and his fellow officers continued north,

deeper into Manchuria, in hopes of finding transportation on the Eastern Railway that connected to the Siberian Railway. It was another five arduous days on foot before they reached Harbin. A Russian stronghold, Harbin had the appearance of a European town with industrial buildings, churches, boulevards, parks—even a theater. Yet, it lacked a welcomed warmth.

Roman found lodging and took advantage of a bath and a hot meal of borscht and Syrniki pancakes. The warmth of the food and the soothing water washed away the weariness of the journey. He sent Kira a telegram, feeling rejuvenated and ready to confront the challenges that lay ahead.

> MEET ME IN MOSCOW – (STOP)
> MUCH LOVE – (STOP)
> R

ROMAN WAS GLAD to leave this dark and exceptionally cold city. Accommodations on the Chinese train were adequate, although Roman was forced to sleep sitting upright. The journey to catch the Siberian train would take a few days and possibly another week before he reached Moscow. Eager for home, Roman's soul was filled with anticipation as he daydreamed about seeing Kira and Anya. *Anya should be walking by now and growing into a little miss. After the chaos of this war, I can't wait to be surrounded by the love of my family.* Fatigued from the foot trek and ravages of a failed conflict, Roman slept for most of the trip.

THE TRAIN PULLED into Chita in time for Roman to catch the Siberian Railway the same day. The accommodations were of a higher standard than the last train. This had sleeping, food, and chapel cars. He met up again with his fellow officers and joined them in a game of cards.

One of the men spoke. "I heard some soldiers talking in another car. They said the Imperial Guards had suppressed protesters who advanced on the Winter Palace."

Roman thought about those he had trained under him, who were still in the guard.

"They said it was a bloody scene. Defenseless women and children were slaughtered."

We will never be rid of man's inhumanity to man. Roman hoped his fellow musketeers had not participated. He remembered that the Tsar and his family no longer resided at the Winter Palace but were secluded in Selo.

Another man spoke, "The people are starving. There is a shortage of food and supplies, and while all this is going on, he's building another palace in the southern region." He shook his head with disapproval. "I can sympathize with the peasants' plight, but I harbor doubts about Lenin's claims and don't see how writing a constitution will remedy the situation as most can't read."

"I sense storm clouds of turmoil will soon blow in," Roman said.

The train stopped with a jolt, not a rare occurrence.

Interruptions were commonplace to move something out of the way or realign skewed tracks. However, the train had been stationary for an inordinate amount of time. Roman sensed something was wrong. He looked toward the horizon and saw they were still on the eastern side of the Urals. He opened the window, stuck his head out, and glanced toward the engine to see several men gathered around. *I wonder what's going on.*

The train door opened with a crash, and four men with guns entered. They swaggered in with bold indifference on their unmasked faces. Roman's body stiffened. He recognized one of them. The familiar face sat next to him and flipped his cards over.

"I see you are losing, brother."

"What in the hell are you doing here, Artie?"

Artie tilted the brim of his hat up with the gun barrel. "It's like this. We've been slaving over this railway without pay and with very little food. So, the boys and I decided we'd had enough. We reckon this railway owes us. That's why we're here. Now because you're my brother, we won't take anything from you, but the rest of these gents, they're going to have to give it up."

Roman handed over his money. "If you don't take it, they will." Roman nodded to the others sitting at the table. The men nodded back in agreement.

"You know you won't get away with this."

"Brother, Siberia is a vast land with very little rule."

"Where are you headed?"

"If I told you then you'd be forced to tell the law and we can't have that."

The train whistle blew two short toots.

"Must go."

"Take care of yourself."

"I'll be seeing you, brother." Artie gave a mock salute, and the bandits left.

A long whistle and jerk of the car let them know they were on the move again.

"Nice brother," one of the men said sarcastically.

"Actually … he is." Roman revealed a sly smile.

NINETEEN

1905

THE TRAIN PULLED into the Moscow station in the late morning. The sun cast a warm glow on the platform. Kira spotted Roman disembarked and raced into his arms. Masha moseyed over with Anya perched on her hip.

"I've waited an eternity to have your arms around me," Kira said. She felt the thinness of his emaciated body. "We've missed you terribly."

Roman loosened her grip to catch his breath. "How did you know I'd be on this train?"

"We have met every eastern train …" Kira covered her mouth and expelled several dry coughs, "… since I received your telegram."

"Are you all right?" Roman said.

"Remnants of a mere cold."

"A cold." Masha rolled her eyes. "More of a severe

case of pneumonia. Thank goodness, she was staying with me. We have the finest doctors in Moscow, but it was her own fortitude and strong constitution that saved her."

Roman faced Kira straight on. "Why didn't you tell me?"

"I didn't want to worry you. Besides, I'm better now that you're home." She snuggled her face in his chest.

Roman kissed her on top of her head. "I promise to never leave you and Anya again."

"I intend to hold you to that promise," Kira said.

Roman reached out to touch Anya, but she sheltered her face in Masha's shoulder. "She has forgotten me."

"Give her time. She will come around. Let's go home." Kira pulled at Roman's arm to follow her. "Masha has arranged a nice lunch."

"Good. I'm starved for decent food." Roman waved goodbye to his fellow travelers and then climbed into the carriage.

THAT EVENING, AFTER Anya had been put to bed, the three adults sat in the parlor sipping cordials.

"We've heard reports that the war in the Far East did not go well," Masha said. "There is a rumor that General Stessel is facing court-martial charges for cowardice for surrendering Port Arthur."

"I'm not surprised."

"The people are outraged over the amount of

money spent on the war only to lose to the Japanese. The Tsar is under immense pressure to turn over the government to elected representatives."

"Something must be done to quell the uprising or we will certainly have a revolution," Roman said. "And I don't see how a revolution will help the starving and homeless. Not to mention the status quo."

Kira started to cry.

"What's wrong?"

"What does the future hold for Anya? What will become of us ... of all of this?" She waved her hand around the room. "I'm so distraught thinking about the upheaval we are up against."

Roman wiped Kira's tears. "Let's not think about that tonight. Let's enjoy our drinks and good company."

Before the Pavlovitch family traveled to St. Petersburg, Masha gave Roman and Kira a night at the Metropol Hotel and tickets to Vincenzo Belllini's opera *Puritani* at the Bolshoi Theatre. Kira believed her aunt wanted alone time with her great-niece.

ONCE HOME OUTSIDE of St. Petersburg, Roman focused on his family and grappling with his identity in the face of a changing society and political landscape. Witnessing the Army's withdrawal at the enemy's hands left a rancid taste. Would he remain in the regiment or seek a different line of work? *But what do I know other than being a soldier?* He combed his fingers through his hair.

Roman made plans to reunite with Uri, Boris, and

Fëdor. He arranged for them to meet at a local tavern. He was the first to arrive and ordered a bottle of vodka and four glasses. Moments later, his fellow musketeers charged into the room. Uri grabbed Roman with a firm embrace. The others provided a warm handshake and slap on the back.

Roman handed each a filled glass. "All for one and one for all."

They swilled their drinks, and Roman refilled each glass. "So what have I missed?"

"Boris is engaged," Uri said as they all sat.

Roman slapped Boris on the back. "Congratulations. Anyone, I know?"

"It was a family arrangement with a Count's daughter," Boris said. "She is someone I've known since childhood. It was expected." He shrugged.

"And what about you, Fëdor?"

Boris and Uri roared with laughter. "He is destined to remain a bachelor," Boris said.

Fëdor showed no sign of disagreement. He simply lifted his nose in the air.

"You are in the same company as Uri. He also seems to prefer bachelorhood." Roman said.

"It's just that you found the perfect one." Uri swallowed his drink.

Roman furrowed his brow for a quick moment but shrugged it off.

"We heard about the Far East. Devastating." Uri fell back in his chair.

"The Navy is all but gone." Roman shook his head. "I believe people will begin to turn against the Tsar." Roman gulped his shot. "Strikes have become commonplace. We must offer the masses the opportunity to express their desires and demands, or I fear we will lose this country to the revolutionaries."

"You are talking about parliamentary government," Boris said. "You are trying to make us European. We are Russian." He banged his fist on the table.

"I suppose you took part in the slaughter of unarmed women and children in the name of the monarchy."

Boris turned his head away.

"My God, Boris, these people are the backbone of this country. They are Russia." Roman slapped his hand on the table. "Aristocracy is outdated."

Boris jumped from his seat, knocking over his chair. He marched to the door and slammed it shut behind him. Fëdor chewed on his mustache with an apprehensive gaze.

"Roman, you realize that you have severed your relationship with Boris," Uri said.

"I know, but he needs … we all need to be aware of what we are up against."

"War has changed you, Roman."

"It has changed many of us."

TWENTY

1906

ROMAN SAT AT the kitchen table and announced, "I've decided to plant rye grain on our small acreage. It's still early enough in the year to plow and sow, it should allow us enough income through the winter. We will know by then, if we can sustain a living as farmers."

Kira plated breakfast and served him and Anya. "If that's what you've decided," she said with uncertainty. "Anya and I will do what we can to help."

"I don't want to invest in machinery in case this experiment doesn't work. I spoke to one of the locals, Yegor. He is willing to help me for food."

"What if we can't make it? What then? Anya will be eight in a few years, and we will need to send her to boarding school to further her education and develop relations with high society."

"Not to worry, dear. We will be fine." Roman

hoped his measured words would soothe her concerns."

Kira kept her thoughts to herself. *Even though Roman dislikes my speaking of my dowry, I can always use it for Anya.*

IVAN, ROMAN'S CALVARY horse, was too old and not built for a plow. Instead, Roman purchased an ox. By the end of the first week of tilling, Roman felt he had aged ten years, yet he still had several weeks of planting ahead of him. The dirt caked under his nails, and his black-stained knuckles reminded him why every muscle ached. He could hardly make a fist for the burning blisters on his palms. Kira took out one of her sewing needles and punctured his blisters to let a torrent of fluid drain. She applied ointment and covered his hands with cloth bandages.

"Are you certain you're up to farming?" She smiled and kissed his forehead.

"Right now, I just want to sleep and dream we are vacationing at the seaside."

"Oh, Papa, can we go to the sea? I so want to swim and let the tiny fish nibble my toes."

"Someday, Anya, someday." But he knew that day might not come soon—if at all.

FOR THE NEXT several weeks, Roman continued to toil in the field. Planting went slower than he had hoped due to the periodical rest he needed because of his old breathing injury. Kira planted a vegetable garden of potatoes and cabbage. She tried to elicit Anya's help, but the girl was nowhere to be found. When Kira tried to educate Anya on proper etiquette, her daughter's thoughts were elsewhere. Having a strong bond with her father, Anya preferred the company of her papa. When Kira complained to Roman about Anya's lack of compliance, Roman brushed it aside with a grunt.

Roman and Yegor rested in the field and ate their lunch of boiled potatoes with peas, carrots, pickles, and a piece of meat.

"Sir," Yegor hesitated, "do you hear about what's happening in the Capital?"

"Not much. Why?"

"We had person in the village who could read, but he has died. He used to read the events to us. Before we heard that factory workers, clerks, even servants were on strike. We no longer receive the news."

"I try not to bother myself with such things," Roman said.

"Change is coming. I can feel it."

Roman shrugged.

"Some are thinking of leaving for America. We hear things are better there. People have all the food they can eat, fancy clothes, big homes with a flush toilet in the house, and everyone drives automobiles."

"You think they don't have poor people?"

"I hear even the poor live as kings."

Roman looked toward the house and saw Kira waving at him. A tall figure stood next to her. Roman shaded his eyes to better see. It was Uri.

Uri approached. "How's farming?" He barely contained his laughter. "I'll say one thing." He held his snicker. "You look like hell, old man."

"If there is a place worse than hell, I'm there."

"You should come back to the guard. Everyone misses you. I know you could acquire your old company back."

"I made a promise to Kira that I'd never leave the two of them again."

"Nevertheless, the post is there if you change your mind."

Roman looked toward his field. "You see that." He pointed. "I cultivated it. It's mine and no one can take it from me."

"All right, Roman." Uri patted him on the back. "I stopped by to let you know I will be away for several weeks. We are off to the Tsar's hunting palace somewhere on the outskirts of Belarus. He is bringing several family members and honored guests. Should be quite a ballyhoo." Uri rolled his eyes. "It's some sort of celebration after we thwarted a coup d'état from some members of the Duma. However, the pig war in Serbia has yet to be resolved."

"Pig war, what's that?"

"You've been away too long. It's some kind of trade blockade between guns and pork. The Hapsburgs have imposed it on Serbia. I don't trust those Hapsburgs. They are bound to get us into a war."

"That's exactly why I choose to stay here."

"Don't think for a moment if there is a war that you won't be called upon. Anyway, I've got to get back. I'll see you when I return."

"Good hunting." Roman waved him off with Uri's words of recruitment ringing in his ears.

Kira sidled next to Roman. "Uri will be away for some time," he said.

"Yes, Uri told me." She rested her head against Roman's shoulder.

"He seems to confide in you a lot."

"He's a good friend. He watched over us while you were in the Far East. Made certain we had enough to eat and medicine if needed." She paused. "Are you jealous?"

"He's a great friend, but he is also a man without a wife."

HARVEST BEGAN IN early autumn. Roman and Yegor sickled the grain in less than a week. Afterward, he had the locals bring their cattle over to graze on the stubble and fertilize the field for the next season.

The crop was bountiful, yielding enough money to survive the winter and into the following year. But Roman had not counted on the high taxes imposed by the Tsar. Taxes that crush any hope of prosperity for the peasantry. He now more than ever understood their plight. *The peasants are being sacrificed not for modern industrialization but to fill the pockets of the elite.* He realized farming was not a feasible way to sustain a living. Once again, he had to determine the course of his family's future.

TWENTY-ONE

1907-1908

BEFORE THE END of winter, Roman and Kira made a pivotal decision. They realized the relentless struggle to sustain a living off the land was improbable. Roman sold the property for less than its value, and they moved into the city. Kira was happy to leave the farm after witnessing the toll it took on Roman's health.

Roman took up Uri's offer and returned to the military. However, he did not return to his old guard unit. Still held in esteem by the Romanovs, Roman had the good fortune to select his assignment. He decided on the training center, where he managed young cadets with riding classes, sword fighting, and rifle practice.

The family found a cozy two-bedroom apartment with a picturesque view overlooking the Neva River. Kira was overjoyed about the new living space, especially the inglenook fireplace that would lend to warm evenings during the bitter cold winter months. She was happy that Anya had adjusted to the move even though she missed the farm.

Living in the city, they were surrounded by a vibrant energy a stark contrast to the quiet farm life they once knew. The bustling streets, vibrant markets, and myriad of cultural events were a testament to the city's liveliness. They extended a standing invitation for Friday night dinners. Uri always attended. Fëdor popped in occasionally. Rumors abounded that Fëdor was romancing a young woman. Boris never responded to the invitation. Uri told Roman his last harsh words to Boris, still burned in his obstinate heart.

AN UNEXPECTED KNOCK at the door disrupted Roman's reading of Tolstoy's *A Calendar of Wisdom*. "Who could that be?" Roman grumbled. He stood frozen at the doorway. A gasp slipped past his lips. "How did you find me?"

"They know where you live," Artie said. He entered the flat without an invitation. "They know where everyone lives."

"Who are they?" Roman shut the door.

"The people who want to change the world. They keep tabs on anyone affiliated with the Romanovs."

Roman grabbed his brother's arm. "Artie, what are you mixed up in?"

Artie jerked his arm free. "Nothing … yet."

"I suppose they know you're here?"

"How do you think I found you?"

Roman felt the blood drain from his face. His first thought was to get Kira and Anya out of St. Petersburg.

"Don't worry. They won't hurt you or your family."

Kira entered the parlor with Anya by her side. "What about the family?"

Roman said. "Artie was asking about where you and Anya were and here you are." He eyed his brother.

"Oh, so you're Roman's brother. I have heard very little about you." She smiled at Roman.

"Not much to tell." Artie bent forward. "And who's this little princess?"

"Anya, this is your Uncle Artie," Kira said. Anya curtsied as she had been taught. "You're just in time for supper. Anya and I will set the table while you two catch up."

Artie relaxed on the chaise longue while Roman paced the floor.

"What are you doing here?"

"To see you, my brother."

"Seriously."

"Yes, seriously. I met a man who also spent time in Siberia. His tactics are extreme but his passion to better the lives of everyday people gets attention. He's about my age, a sturdy-looking Georgian with a mean glint and a monstrous head of hair." He laughed.

"What's his name?"

"Something no one can pronounce. He goes by Joe. He's the money man."

"What does that mean?"

"He helps finance the cause, although I'm sure through unscrupulous means."

"You mean robbery."

No response.

"Supper is ready," Kira announced.

ROMAN AND URI sat in the parlor late one night, smoking cigars and drinking cognac.

"We've arrested several left-wing politicians and activists in the last several months," Uri said. "In fact, one of their ringleaders escaped to Switzerland. That should put a crimp in any more uprisings."

Roman thought about Artie. "They seem very determined and their numbers are growing."

"Roman, you sound like an anarchist." Uri puffed on his cigar. "There's talk of an alliance between England and France."

"That will surely upset the Germans." A knock at the door interrupted their conversation. "I'll be right back."

Roman opened the door to see Artie bent over and holding his side. A trace of blood seeped through his fingers. Roman's thoughts raced to Uri in the next room. He pulled Artie inside and headed around the corner to the kitchen. "I'll be right with you, Uri."

Kira had just put Anya to bed and was cleaning up after supper when the two entered the kitchen. She stood silent, away from the sink, her hands dripping soapy water.

Roman removed Artie's hand to see what appeared to be a knife wound. He whispered to Kira, "Quick, get me a towel." He placed it on the laceration. "Now hold this tight." His voice became severe. "Of all the times to show up. I've got an Imperial Guard sitting in the parlor."

"Who do you think stabbed me? We were marching peacefully when they rode up and started slashing their swords about."

"Never mind, I don't want to hear anymore. Kira, do what you can. I will try and get Uri to leave." Roman made his way back to the parlor.

"Who was at the door this late at night?" Uri said.

"One of Kira's lady friends. She dropped off laundered cloths." Roman faked a yawn. "It's getting late. Do you mind if we continue this conversation another time?"

"All right old man." Uri finished drink and rose from the chair. "I'll just say goodnight to Kira."

A cold shiver of anxiety ran through Roman's body. "No. I mean, she has already gone to bed."

"Very well then, goodnight."

Roman returned to the kitchen. Artie's head was resting on the table. "How is he?"

Kira's voice was shaking. "He needs a doctor."

"You can't." Artie eked out, "I'll be arrested."

"Oh, Roman, what do we do?"
"If we can't take him to a hospital. Then there's only one other place.

TWENTY-TWO

1908-1909

ROMAN TENDERLY HOISTED his half-conscious brother out of the carriage and carried him into Ivan's barn. He had sent Kira to fetch the veterinarian. The once-white towel used to suppress the torrent of blood from Artie's injury was now soaked red.

Ivan whinnied and kicked up his hind legs. Roman tied him up at the far end of the stall to avoid an accidental hoof stomp.

"Sorry, brother." Artie winced.

Roman soothed Artie's brow. "We may have our differences, but you're still my brother."

"I didn't mean for you to get caught up in my world."

"It's the times we live in. I don't think any of us in good conscience can turn our backs on what's happening in front of us."

"Do you mean to say you are with us, brother?

Roman shook his head. "I understand the plight of the peasant, but I don't believe that those who wish to overthrow the government will bring those in need any solace."

Artie's body went limp. His eyes closed.

Roman felt time moved languidly as he waited for the veterinarian.

When the vet finally arrived, he rubbed Ivan's long, coarse mane. "Now, what's the matter with my handsome fellow?"

"That's not the patient." Roman tapped the vet's shoulder.

The vet turned and recoiled to see an unconscious man lying on the stall floor. "What is this?"

"He's my brother. He needs your help."

"I'm not a medical doctor."

"I've seen you do miracles on Ivan. You are as good as any medical doctor."

The vet stood motionless.

"Please." Roman's voice cracked with desperation. "I don't want him to go to prison ... or worse."

The doctor patted Roman on the back. "I'll do what I can, but no promises." He knelt and pulled back the towel to reveal a thin V-shaped line on the abdomen where the sword's blade penetrated. "It doesn't appear to have penetrated any organs. I'll need to sew up the blood vessel and flesh." He pulled out an antiseptic from his bag to clean the wound and started stitching. Artie regained consciousness and began to thrash about. The doctor placed a chloroform cloth over his nose and mouth to quiet him.

The doctor rose to his feet. "He'll need several days of rest." He handed Roman a pillbox. "Give him one a day for the pain. I'll stop by the apartment in a couple of days to check on him and remove the stitches."

"I need your report to say that you treated Ivan for colic."

The veterinarian nodded.

ARTIE SAT AT the kitchen table. Since the stitches had been removed, he was able to walk around the apartment, albeit with a cane.

Anya twirled around the room until she got dizzy and fell.

"I see Anya had a good time from the palace's invitation," he said.

"Yes." Kira wiped a few loose hairs from her face and sat. Anya continued to twirl. "Anya, be still or go to your room." Kira gave her a disapproving glare.

When Kira looked away, Anya twirled again.

"I see you."

Artie winced as he lifted and placed Anya on his lap. "How was it, princess?"

"We played with the most beautiful dolls," Anya chimed in. "They have the most wonderful dollhouse with different levels and tiny tables, chairs, beds—just like a real house."

"It was very nice," Kira said. "The older girls sewed elaborately trimmed clothing for the dolls."

Anya slid off Artie's legs and approached her mother. "Maria is my favorite."

Kira stroked her daughter's hair. "Yes, dear. Now, go change your clothes." She scooted her away with a pat on her backside.

"How is it that you were invited?" Artie said.

"I met the Tsarina while Roman and I were in Crimea. She remembered me and that I had a girl about the same age as her younger daughters. The Duchesses are very sweet. Anastasia is a bit mischievous, but Maria has a quiet reverence with magnetic blue eyes that pierce your soul." Kira paused to reflect. "They are a lovely family."

Kira saw Artie's pursed lips holding back his disapproval. She ignored it, rose from her seat, and prepared the evening meal. "I wish for my country to return to the old ways. The ways of my childhood— for Anya's sake."

"It's too late for wishing. The present is ours and we plan to build a bright new future."

"ANYA IS DOWN for the night and Artie is resting in his bedroom." Kira cocked her head to the side. "What's the matter? You walked in the door tonight with a scowl and it hasn't diminished."

Roman rubbed his chin, stretched back, and placed his hands behind his head. "I don't want Artie to hear about this."

Kira nodded.

"They've launched a recruitment campaign in the last several weeks. The Tsar has it in his head to expand into more territory."

"Isn't that good for your position?"

"This is not the time for annexation. I don't see how he can afford it, given the amount of gold and cash that was recently seized by the Bolsheviks."

"You mentioned earlier that the Germans were building forces. Maybe he's being prudent."

Roman unlaced his fingers and sat forward. "If war breaks out, it could fuel the socialists and civil conflict will tear this country apart. I fear for you and Anya, especially in light of the chief of police's assassination."

"What do you propose?"

"I spoke with Captain Kolchak. I served with him at Port Arthur. He's to be stationed in Vladivostok. He has invited me to assist him in an Arctic exploration. It might mean a possible relocation. If nothing else, it would be a way to avoid the inevitable turmoil on this side of the Urals."

"I worry about taking Anya away from Russian society."

"Kira, have you not been listening to me? Russian society is collapsing all around us." He paused to take a breath. "This is a way for us to remain together. Kolchak said there are theaters where they perform ballet and chamber music. They have an elegant hotel where we can dine out. There is even a girl's school. The city is a cosmopolitan blend of different cultures."

Kira fidgeted with her hair. "Whatever you think, dear."

"We'll need to put on a front and continue to attend social events such as the theater and balls. I will see about arranging a transfer. But first, we need to get my brother out of the house."

TWENTY-THREE

1910

ROMAN STOOD AT the parlor window and watched the steamship pilot navigate the river. Below, horse-drawn carts loaded with fresh supplies were off to places unknown. Vendors sold goods from their kiosks lined up along the port to a crowd of raggedy-dressed people in search of a daily meal.

"Peasants continue to plow and sow their fields by hand in hopes of a good crop. During harvest, the women sickle and bundle the grain, the men beat the wheat to release the seed, and then send it off to the mill. City folk stand in line for a loaf of bread that the farmer can barely afford." Roman shook his head. "The dogs owned by the upper class are fed better than the people."

Kira stood beside Roman, rubbed his back, and rested her head on his shoulder.

"Look at the sky. The mass of factories chokes the city with billowing black smoke. Their only purpose is to produce the materials to build warships." Roman turned and wrapped an arm around Kira. "Unmasked miners mine for ore that fills their lungs with dust for a few rubles.

Kira said, "It's no wonder the people march along the streets in protest."

"And the Tsar and his family continue to parade around the city with the children in tow, escorted by the military. He is so stubbornly blind. Uri says that the threats against the Tsar's life have increased, yet he believes the people still worship and adore him. And believe me, he is not God."

"Can't someone talk to him?"

"There is no one who can change the course. He dismisses anyone who disagrees with him. Or they simply get frustrated and resign."

"We will be gone soon and we can leave this all behind us."

"The country is sick and the illness will certainly spread." He patted Kira's hand. "But we will be safe far away from the hypocrisy."

"Your promotion to Major should come through soon …"

"Promotion," Roman laughed. "Most of the battle-ready, high-ranking officers from the last war died a few years ago. The only reason they plan to give it to me is because they fear I might leave. Once it happens, we can make our plans to move to Vladivostok."

"I've asked Artie to come with us, but he refuses. He wishes to stay and fight for a new Russia. I don't know what's to become of him. His new friends are an unsound influence. I fear one friend puts Artie in dangerous situations. His wound just healed and he's off storming the streets again. I fear he might be involved in setting off bombs. Or worse."

"Artie is a man who must do what he must do. Just as we must."

Roman turned to leave.

"The river will freeze soon and the racing and theatre season will begin. I will need to order new dresses and hats from Paris."

Roman faced Kira. "Do you hear yourself?"

Kira placed her hands on her hips. "What am I supposed to do? Give my sable and dresses to the poor? Besides, you said we must maintain a façade until we leave."

Roman walked away and mumbled, "It can't be soon enough."

THE WINTER SOLSTICE had passed, and the Neva River was frozen. The Pavlovitch family watched the automobile races from their bay window. Outside, bundled-up onlookers with fur-lined caps crowded alongside the makeshift ice track, urging on their favorites.

"Look, Papa. There are even motorbikes racing."

"One has skis attached to the tires," Kira laughed.

They watched as the vehicles skidded around the ice. The open-topped autos were loaded with four to six people, mainly used for stabilization. One vehicle spun out of control and slid into the crowd, knocking over several people.

Anya buried her face in Roman's chest.

"Look, Anya. Everyone is getting back on their feet. They're all right."

Anya slowly pulled her head away to see for herself.

"How about some hot chocolate?" Kira said.

"Oh, yes please." Anya bounced up and down.

"Ladies don't bounce," Kira said. "I'll put a little extra something in yours." She winked at Roman.

Roman and Anya continued to watch the race. "I want the blue one with four people," Anya said. "Which one are you rooting for?"

"Um, I think I like that one too."

"Oh, Papa. You have to pick a different one so we can see which one of us wins."

"Very well. I choose the motorbike."

They cheered for their picks. A rich-sweet scent filled the room when Kira returned with a tray of hot chocolate.

Suddenly, the motorbike skidded on its side and slammed into a snowbank. Anya's pick sped across the finish line.

Anya jumped up and clapped and yelled, "I win. I win, I win."

Kira whispered to Roman. "I will miss the City."

ROMAN AND KIRA approached the Mariinsky Theatre's grand façade adorned with alabaster columns. They climbed the sweeping staircase and entered their box seats. Roman took Kira's coat to reveal her recent Paris purchase of a gold damask gown with a blue chiffon sash and gold florets. Tassel fringe hung below the beaded bodice.

The opulent theatre interior had a gilded ceiling with equally gilded balconies. Kira took her opera glasses and searched the rich velvet seats on the main floor.

"Who are you looking for?" Roman said.

"Uri. You said he's escorting a woman. I want to see who she is."

Roman rolled his eyes and picked up his program.

"There he is." Kira paused to study the woman beside Uri. "She's rather plain-featured."

Roman looked through his program. "I am looking forward to this production of *Giselle*. This maybe the last time to see Anna Pavolva. After all, she is getting on in years."

"I want to go meet them during intermission."

"Yes, dear."

The overhead lights dimmed. The orchestra leader tapped his baton on the music stand and raised his arms to begin Adolphe Adam's opening score.

At intermission, Kira and Roman made their way to the main floor. They snaked their way through the crowd, acknowledging several acquaintances with a nod or short greeting as they passed by.

Kira approached Uri first. "Hello." They kissed each other on both cheeks.

"You look lovely tonight," Uri said.

"You're too kind." Kira eyed Uri's female companion and smiled but addressed Uri. "Congratulations on your promotion. A captain now."

"Thank you, but I'm still below this guy." Uri nudged Roman.

"Roman, Kira, this is Mademoiselle Lada." Uri's cheeks flushed. His eyes darted at each one of them.

Kira eyed Lada's dress. She suspected it was from a shop, not couture.

Lada shifted her stance.

The bell rang to notify everyone to return to their seats.

"You must join us on Sunday at the races," Kira said as they left.

When they returned to their box, Roman said, "I hope you won't be so rude on Sunday."

"What did I say?"

"You scrutinized her, which made her feel uncomfortable."

"I did not," Kira lied. "Anyway, she isn't as plain as at first glance." She turned her attention to the stage

THAT SUNDAY, THE four met at the snow-covered equestrian racetrack. The event was attended by various gentry of people. Box seats reserved near the judge's stand were for the nobility and high dignitaries. Roman was able to secure seats a few rows away. Women dressed in red finery dazzled the grandstand. The band played music as the race began.

Kira was careful not to examine Lada, but she wanted to know all about this woman. "Do you live with your family in the city?"

"We live near the university. My father is a mathematics professor."

"Mathematics … how nice." Kira feigned interest. Wanting more intimate details. She inquired, "I'd love to know how you and Uri met." Roman elbowed her, but she ignored him.

"Kira, your horse is nearing the finish line," Roman said.

"My husband thinks I'm being rude. You don't mind my questions, do you?"

"Not at all. We met at a mutual friend's house party."

Kira turned her attention to Uri, who was watching the race. Still, she suspected he was listening to their conversation as his cheeks were flushed.

The horses rounded the last corner. Men and women waved their handkerchiefs as the horses approached the finish line.

Roman said. "Let's all go for a nice warm drink."

Everyone nodded.

Kira took Lada's arm as they walked. "I wish we could get to know you better, but we will be leaving the city soon."

"Kira!" Roman said.

"What's this," Uri said. "Where are you going?"

TWENTY-FOUR

KIRA'S PARENTS ARRIVED in St. Petersburg two days before the Pavlovitch family were to leave for Moscow. Roman and Kira saw the visible distress on her parents' faces regarding their impending move to Vladivostok. They decided to spend the last few days in a hotel with Kira's parents to strengthen their bond as a family.

After a day of her mother's tears, Kira wished the time to leave for Moscow would come soon. "I've never seen her so emotional. My nerves are starting to fray. I think Anya is in sympathy and tries to amuse Mother with long stories. The stories seem to go in circles with no end but Mother just nods and says 'that's nice, dear,'" Kira said.

Roman grabbed his coat and headed for the door. "I need to speak with Uri."

"Will you be long? It's better when you are here. Mother feels the need to tell me her troubles when you are absent. I can't hear one more account of Father's drinking and philandering."

Roman kissed Kira on the forehead. "Steady on. We will be leaving tomorrow."

THE PUNGENT SMELL of horse manure and urine mixed with hay, filled Roman's nostrils as he brushed Ivan's long black mane. "We need to make you a handsome boy." Roman felt a lump creeping up in his throat. He swallowed it back.

Uri strolled into the stable. "I can't believe you're really leaving."

Roman's lips slid to one side. "It wasn't a decision made lightly," he sighed. He continued to brush Ivan's coat. "I gave him a long run this morning. He'll need another run in a few days. The vet says he's in good shape and I've had him shod recently." Roman's hands trembled as he caressed Ivan's muzzle.

"He'll be well cared for, Roman. I promise."

Roman wrapped his arms around Ivan, buried his head in his freshly combed mane, and wept. When he let go, Ivan whinnied and nudged Roman with his head. Roman handed the reins to Uri. He patted the horse. "You behave, ol' boy." He wiped his eyes. "I feel as though I'm giving my son away." His voice choked with emotion. Roman turned, his shoulders slumped, and strolled out of the stable.

"Write once in a while." Uri's voice echoed. "Let us know how you and Kira are doing."

Roman continued walking, raised his right arm, and waved. Each step a struggle against the weight of his feelings.

ALEXANDER HAD ARRANGED to treat everyone to a meal in a lavish hotel. Kira thought the dining room's low lighting fashioned a romantic elegance. They were seated in a private burgundy velvet-drape booth.

Roman pulled on his shirt collar like an expected groom. Anya fidgeted in her chair. To Kira, it summoned thoughts of da Vinci's *The Last Supper*. She believed it to be the last time she would experience anything this lavish. *I'm certain they won't have anything this refined in the Far East.*

The table wobbled. Kira touched Anya's leg to stop her from swinging them. "Sit up, dear."

"Mother, I can't eat this. It looks icky."

"Did you try it?"

Anya twisted her lips.

"It's mushroom soup. Try it, dear. If you don't care for it, leave it and they will take it away."

Anya placed a tiny amount of the gray soup on her spoon, touched it with the tip of her tongue, and crinkled her nose. She rested the spoon at an angle at the edge of the soup plate.

"Roman," Alexander said. "When do you think you will arrive in Vladivostok?"

"The trip is less than a fortnight." He paused. "Longer if the train breaks down as it often does."

"We hope to arrive before the first snow," Kira said.

"I hope you have enough warm clothes." Her mother's voice cracked.

"I understand that the weather is similar to Moscow. We'll be fine."

"Roman, what will you be doing out there?" Alexander took a heaping forkful of his Veal Orloff, heavy with mushrooms and béchamel sauce.

"Vladivostok is an active trading port. Several nations come in and out of there. I will assist in securing Russian affairs."

"Kira, you are leaving all of your friends. What will you do?" her mother said.

"I will join a ladies' circle and meet new friends." Kira planted a smile on her face.

Kira's mother leaned into Kira and whispered, "Don't ask too much of your Auntie while you are in Moscow."

Kira furrowed her brow and pursed her lips.

"Masha has been ill of late. I thought you should know."

Kira's mind whirled. *Masha is perfectly fit. She carries on like a woman in her twenties. Mother must be jealous.* Her thoughts tried to console her, but dinner churned in her stomach.

THE TRAIN WHISTLE blew as the last call to board was announced.

"I've tried to reach Artie, but I haven't been able to make contact. I left a message with his landlord.

Hopefully, he can meet us before we leave." Roman stretched his neck above the crowd in search of Artie. "I guess he didn't get my message."

Roman felt a gentle tap on his back. When he turned, a sizeable grin spread across his face. "Artie." He grabbed his brother with an exaggerated embrace. "I'm so glad to see you."

"Of course, Brother. But I don't know why you are leaving. All the excitement is here in St. Petersburg."

"I've witnessed enough excitement."

Artie crouched to Anya's level. "How do you feel about the move, princess?"

Anya cradled her rosy-checked porcelain doll. "I think it will be quite an adventure."

Artie straightened up. "Precocious isn't she."

"At eight, she has a mind of her own," Kira said.

"Good luck to you all. I'm certain you'll be back."

"If we are, it will be for a visit."

They all exchanged goodbye hugs. Kira's mother hugged her tighter than she could remember.

"I fear I will never see you again." Tears welled up in her mother's eyes.

Her father gave Roman a stern look with a furrowed brow and a firm handshake? "Take care of my daughter and granddaughter."

"I assure you Sir, they will have no reason to complain."

Anya kissed and hugged her grandmother and grandfather goodbye.

The three boarded the train and entered their cabin. Roman pulled down the window and they stuck out their heads. Steam billowed above as they wave goodbye. Kira watched her mother cry into her handkerchief as the train left the station. Her father stood stalwart. At that moment, her heart grew heavy. It suddenly occurred to her that it might be years before she saw them again.

TWENTY-FIVE

Masha met the Pavolivich family at the Nikolayevsky railway station. Warm sun rays penetrated from above the arched Palladian windows as the three departed the train. Kira was the first to spot Masha in a lengthy, cream, light-wool dress trimmed with silk lace inlays. She rushed to hug her aunt. As they released their embrace, Kira's eyes fell on the staff Masha was braced against. "What happened?"

"Oh, this. I foolishly fell in the garden last week."

"Are you all right?" Kira recalled what her mother had said about Masha being ill.

"The doctor said something about my balance. What does he know anyway?" Masha kissed Roman on both cheeks. Looking at Anya, she said, "Oh my, how this little one has grown. Do you remember your Auntie Masha?"

Anya held onto her doll in one arm and gripped

the skirt of her mother's dress with the other.

"Let's collect your things. I have a bit of lunch ready at home," Masha said.

Their heels click-clacked across the parquet oak floor of the main hall as they passed through the clock tower to the street, where they encountered the buzz of streetcars, carriages, automobiles, and people scurrying about. A testament to the city's vibrancy. Across the way, a grassy circle held the statue of Tsar Alexander III. Directly in front, Masha's carriage waited for them, a relic of a bygone era.

"Auntie Masha," Anya said. "When are you going to get a horseless buggy?"

"Never, dear. It's simply not a refined way to travel around town."

Kira and Roman smiled at each other and climbed into the carriage.

THAT EVENING, AFTER she and Roman had retired to their bed, Kira said, "Anya needs to experience the culture that Moscow has to offer. I want to show her Saint Basil Cathedral, the Moskovsky Zoopark, and take her to the ballet. Tchaikovsky's *The Sleeping Beauty* is performing at the Bolshoi Theater. I think she is old enough to understand the story. We can use Masha's box seats."

Roman twisted his lips.

Kira laughed. "You don't have to go."

Roman rolled on top of her and kissed her.

AT BREAKFAST, KIRA voiced her plans. "Anya, how about we attend the ballet?"

Anya shrugged.

"It's about a princess who is cursed to sleep for a hundred years by an evil fairy, then awakened by a handsome prince."

"Like the fairy tale that you read to me at night?"

"Exactly. And this morning, we are going to see all the animals at the zoopark."

"Lions and elephants?" Anya's eyes sparkled.

"And many more."

Anya clapped her hands and jumped up and down in her seat.

"Don't jump or clap at the table. Remember, you are a young lady now." Kira turned to her aunt. "Would you care to join us? Later, I plan to take her to Trinity Square to see Saint Basil Cathedral.?"

"Thank you, no. I need to rest my legs. Besides, Roman and I can have a nice long conversation."

Roman gave Kira an expression as if to say, how can I get out of this?

KIRA AND ANYA entered Moskovsky Zoopark. They passed through a castle-like stone structure that revealed a flower garden surrounded by tall trees. Anya spotted the elephants and ran toward their enclosure. A man with a bag of peanuts approached Anya and gave her a nut.

"Hold out your hand and it will take it," he said.

Anya felt the soft skin of the elephant's long trunk gently take the peanut. "It tickles," she giggled.

"Thank you, sir," Kira said. "Alright. Let's go see some of the other animals."

They wandered by the lion enclosures, but the magnificent felines were napping. They passed through the primate habitats where mischievous monkeys swung from ropes, causing Anya to laugh. A solitary male gorilla sat behind a glass enclosure, observing passing visitors.

Anya looked at her mother. "In some ways, it resembles us, doesn't it?"

"Yes, in some … I think it's the eyes." Kira stopped by a vendor's cart and ordered pink Fairy Flosses. Kira handed one to Anya.

"What is it, Mother?"

"Spun sugar. It's a special treat. Come, let's catch the streetcar for the next venture."

ROMAN SAT ON the settee reading, relishing some quiet time alone.

Masha entered the parlor, followed by a servant with a tray of tea and biscuits. Her two Pekingese's long, shiny fur swept across the floor as they panted after her. "What are you reading?"

"The Brothers Karamazov," Roman said without looking up from the book.

"Interesting. Are you looking for answers to your conflicts?"

"No. I borrowed it from Kira. It was given it as a gift. I simply needed something to read on the long journey ahead."

Masha sat, then waved for the servant to leave the room. "Tell me why you feel the need to move so far away." She pinched off pieces of biscuit and fed it to the dogs.

Roman set the book on his lap. "The move provides advancement."

"I would think you could rise in rank closer to home." She poured herself a cup of tea.

"If you must know, I find the unrest in St. Petersburg and here n Moscow dangerous. I want to make certain my family is safe."

"I see. And how do you think our country is going to emerge from this discontent?"

"I'm afraid we will never see the Russia that we've grown to love."

Masha placed her cup on the table. "I fear you are right. But what of Kira? In speaking with her, she has expressed great anxiety over this move."

"She fears the change, the unknown, the lack of her abilities. Once she sees how similar Vladivostok is to this part of the world, her fears will diminish."

"I hope you are right." Her voice had a tone of imprudence.

Roman picked up his book and continued to read. He was eager to immerse himself in the story and avoid further conversation about the move.

KIRA AND ANYA disembarked the tram at Trinity Square. The square was paved in stone, a bustling hub of activity, with vendors selling gifts, goods, and food along the moat in front of the majestic Saint Basil Cathedral. The cathedral revealed its breathtaking onion-domed tops in vibrant hues of blues, reds, yellows, and greens that stood out against the clear azure sky. South of the cathedral lay the Central Fortress, surrounded by crenelated red brick walls, its twenty towers, and the palace.

"What is that?" Anya pointed to the fortress.

"That is where the Tsar and his family live … sometimes."

Kira purchased an interior map of the cathedral that displayed nine separate chapels. As they walked through the long, red brick halls, there was very little natural light. At each intersection, a gaslight was suspended from the ceiling. Each chapel was decorated with elaborate, colorful murals of leaves, flowers, and geometric designs.

"Why is it called Saint Basil?"

She pointed to a plaque. "It says here that Saint Basil was the protector of the poor."

"Why are there so many chapels?"

"Each one is named after a Saint. Each telling a unique story of the faith and devotion. The one we are in is the Chapel of St. Nicholas." They silently gazed at the elaborate altar of painted religious icons.

"Their faces are, I don't know, eerie. It's like they

are about to cry," Anya said.

Kira chuckled. "I believe they are trying to show compassion."

"Mother, can we leave now? I'm getting tired.

ROMAN, KIRA, AND Anya decided to spend a delightful evening at the ballet. Inside the theater, iridescent light was interspersed with gold that cast a magical glow. Bright crimson curtains draped the interior boxes, and the stucco arabesques differed on each floor. The central eye-catcher of the auditorium was a massive three-tiered chandelier consisting of lights and candelabra decorated with crystals.

An usher hurried Roman and Kira to their seats as the music started and the curtain rose. The princess ballerina wore an off-white sleeveless tight bodice and full skirt that extended several yards. Anya squeezed her mother's arm and stared wide-eyed at the stage.

Anya whispered to her mother, "It looks as though they are floating in the air." She remained mesmerized.

At intermission, Kira said, "Anya, what do you think so far?"

"The costumes were wonderful but that evil fairy scares me."

"Don't worry, she'll get her comeuppance."

As the curtain fell ending the performance. Anya shared her favorite part. "I especially loved the fairy who helped them get together."

"And they lived happily ever after," Kira said, with a twinkle in her eye.

The three laughed.

THE FOLLOWING DAY, they arrived at Yaroslavsky railway station for their long journey to the Far East. The family entered the station and was confronted by a man dressed in ragged clothes with a long salt-and-pepper beard. He shouted at passersby that God was coming and they must repent. Roman hurried the family to the station platform to ensure their safety.

Anya stared at the peasant women's weathered faces. The women wore long, dingy skirts. Atop their heads, they wore multi-colored babushkas. Several carried baggage in one hand and lugged a child on a hip as they followed their husbands. Soldiers loaded them onto a car without windows.

"Are they going to Vlad ... Vlad ... you know?" Anya said.

"No. They're off to prison," Roman said.

"Why?"

"They're seditionists."

Anya grabbed her father's hand, hid one eye in his pant leg, and peered at the peasants with the other. "What's sad-tion-ist?"

"People who disagree with the Tsar." Roman took his daughter's hand as they boarded the train headed for Siberia.

TWENTY-SIX

TUCKED AWAY IN their sleeper cabin, Roman and Kira sat on a plush red seat that converted into a bed. A bunk bed hung above their heads. Roman had acquired accommodations with a toilet in their compartment. A stark difference from the Tsar's stylish train they had traveled when returning from Crimea, yet comfortable.

Anya sat snuggled in a corner seat opposite her parents. Her gaze fixated on the countryside. "Mother, look at the horses playing in the field. Their coat is curly not smooth like Ivan's."

"Yes, dear." Kira glanced at Roman, who had a melancholy look on his face. She rubbed his arm, knowing his thoughts lay with his beloved horse.

A knock, then a voice called out from the other side of the door. "Tea, sir."

Roman opened the door and waved in the attendant. A sweet floral fragrance filled the room as the attendant placed the tray on the table. The glass cups were set inside metal holders emblazoned with the Russian Imperial Coat of Arms. The attendant placed two sugar sticks and a lemon slice into each cup. Lemon slices floated to the top of the glass as he poured dark tea from a silver teapot.

Roman said, "When will we arrive in Vyatka?"

"Before dinner, but it will be a short stop, sir." The attendant bowed and left the cabin.

"How much father to Vladivostok?" Anya said.

"Several days, dear. Please don't ask anymore." Kira sipped her tea.

THE SUN'S FIERY orb lingered along the horizon as the train approached Vyatka. The three left the train to embark on a new setting.

"Despite being on solid ground, I still feel a gentle rocking sensation," Kira said.

"Give it time, it will pass," Roman smiled.

Anya's eyes lifted when she spotted colorfully painted clay figures at a kiosk. She picked up a bluebird and showed it to her father. Roman rolled his eyes and paid the merchant. They strolled outside toward the town. In the distance, imposing gray onion-shaped domes from a white cathedral soared above a burnt umber sky. The train's last call whistle sounded, and they headed back.

Anya placed her bird on the cabin table and stoked it. "Pretty bird. I think I'll name her Vasilisa, from the fairy tale."

Kira laid out a pink dress and white socks. "Anya,

please ready yourself for dinner."

"Mother, may I take Vasilisa to dinner?"

Kira thought for a moment. "If you promise to eat all of your vegetables."

Anya scrunched her lips and nodded.

The family strolled down the electrically-lit corridor into the dining car. The tables were placed against gold-draped windows. A design of interlaced wrought iron separated every table. Each table was immaculately set with silverware and glassware according to protocol. Several people seated were already finishing their first course. A steward greeted the Pavlovitch family with a bow and showed them to their table. From the extensive menu, Roman ordered cabbage soup, followed by beet salad, dumplings filled with minced meat slathered in butter and topped with *crème fraiche*, and a layered pastry for dessert. Throughout the meal, glasses of wine and vodka were served. Anya was allowed to drink a small quantity of diluted wine.

IT WAS EARLY morning when the train pulled into the Perm station, a city known for its unique blend of Russian and European architectural styles. They had been informed that the stop would be several hours. After breakfast, the three departed the train to explore the city. They strolled past storefronts along dirt streets with elevated wooden walkways. Single and two-story stately homes were scattered throughout the town. The houses were painted pink, red, or blue, with elaborately carved and milled woodwork surrounding the windows.

"Remember, Anya, no presents," Kira said as they strolled along the walkway.

Anya stuck out her lower lip and dragged her feet.

"Do you have Vasilisa?" Roman said

Anya smiled and pulled the bird from inside her coat pocket.

A rumbling racket a few blocks away caught Roman's attention. Several people angrily marched down the center of the street. Their disgruntled banners read "Bread for Workers." Boisterous declarations resonated with anger.

Anya's eyes opened wide, and she started to shake. "I'm scared, Papa."

Roman gathered up his daughter. "We need to return to the train. Quickly, Kira."

Kira lifted her skirt with one hand to extend her stride and wrapped her other hand around Roman's arm. The family hurried back to safety as the voices of protesters faded into the distance.

KIRA AND ROMAN quelled Anya's fears by distracting her with a fairy story. Within an hour, the train left Perm, paralleling the Kama River. The narrow spine of the mythological Ural mountain range overlooked the red and yellow autumn foliage. The rhythmic clattering of train wheels along the tracks provided a soothing hum, lulling them into a peaceful state. Roman's nose whistled while Kira's breath gurgled as they dozed upright.

Anya stared out the window. "I'm so bored."

Roman opened one eye. "We will be in Asia soon."

"Will we see long braided ponytails and funny clothes?"

Kira picked up her embroidery. "Possibly. But we mustn't make fun of them because they are different."

"Yes, Mother."

"Anya, let's play Durak," Roman said. He shuffled the deck and dealt out six cards. He placed a single card, the ace of diamonds, face up on the table. He stacked the undealt cards face down on top of the trump card but crosswise so that the rank and value remained visible. Anya put down the eight of spades and placed it in the center. Roman played the jack of spades. Anya attacked with a jack of clubs. Roman could not defend and was forced to pick up all the played cards. Anya started a new attack by laying down the eight of spades. They continued to play until she won by playing all the cards in her hand.

"You're the jester, Papa," She laughed.

"It seems so," he chuckled.

AT DINNER, ANYA spotted a new family with a girl close to her age. Her blonde hair was tied back with a wide blue ribbon. She clutched a doll similar to Anya's.

"Mother, may I introduce myself?"

"Yes, dear. But don't intrude if they are still eating." Kira watched her daughter approach the stranger's table. Anya's conversation was directed to the girl.

The child's parents looked up in acknowledgment and waved Roman and Kira over. After the introductions and several vodkas, it was revealed that the father was also a military man ordered to Novonikolayevsk to recruit Cossacks.

"Those Cossacks are good warriors," the man said. "They will help quell the uprising back home."

Roman nodded, careful not to voice his opinion.

Kira changed the subject by addressing the woman, "The girls are getting along nicely. Dolls seemed to unite them. Maybe we could pass out dolls to the military."

The woman laughed. "Good idea. I am so happy the girls have found each other. It's been difficult to constrain my daughter's energy. Sitting and looking at the landscape lasts only so long."

"Yes." Kira agreed.

Roman yawned and rose. "It's getting late." He ushered Kira and Anya back to their cabin. Roman uttered under his breath so Anya could not hear. "He is one of those who believe that they can annihilate the uprising with brutality. All it will do is antagonize the protesters, giving their cause strength and possibly increased ranks."

THE FOLLOWING AFTERNOON, Roman sat engrossed in his book while Kira stitched her linen embroidery. Their peaceful moment was interrupted by the voices of children and a gentle knock at the door. Roman rose and opened the door to find the porter accompanied by Anya and her friend.

"I'm sorry to disturb you, sir," the porter said. "The children have been running up and down the corridor and we've had multiple complaints."

Roman ushered the girls inside. "Thank you, we'll manage it from here." He shut the door and pointed to the corner chair. "You two sit." He placed a deck of cards on the table. "Play … quietly."

Kira said, "Anya, you told me you would be in your friend's cabin."

"We were but we were told we were too noisy and asked to go to the lounge."

Moments later, there was another knock. "Now what?" Roman muttered.

On the other side of the door stood the girl's father. "Ah, there you are. You need to come for tea." He waved his daughter to follow him. He spoke to Roman, "We will see you later tonight."

Roman nodded. The obedient child dropped her cards and left with her father.

Anya sat with her arms crossed and stared at the horizon as the train rattled past a forest of spruce, fir, pine, and birch. Autumn was in full force, with leaves turning from green to shades of red, yellow, and orange. "What's that?" She pointed to a boat with an immense red paddlewheel that propelled it up the river. A plume of steam emitted from tall black vertical stacks.

"Steamboat," Roman said. "That paddlewheel drives the boat. It's used to transport people and goods up and down the river."

They passed a village of mud huts with thatched roofs. Anya noticed the people looked different. They had thick black hair and dark almond eyes. "Papa, are we in Asia?"

THE TRAIN ROLLED into Novonikolayevsk. Anya watched from the cabin window as her friend departed the train, clutching her mother's hand. Anya sighed as they waved goodbye to each other. She picked up her doll and placed it on her lap. "It's just the two of us again."

Roman had made excuses at dinner to not linger with the couple but had wished them good luck on their travels. He noticed that they were met by a man dressed in a fur hat. He wore a long blue coat with wide flared sleeves. Several knives were secured to his waistband. "Cossack," he muttered. *I hope Artie had the good sense to leave St. Petersburg before reinforcements arrived, but I know my wish will go unheeded.*

THE NEXT STOP was Tayshet, a station nestled along the River Angara. A short walk across a bridge took one to the city center, but not for those in the last car. The dissidents who boarded in Moscow were being offloaded like cattle.

Anya watched intently as men with rifles herded the people. "Where are they taking them?"

"A work camp," Roman said.

"What is that?"

"A harsh place." Roman did not want to explain to his impressionable daughter the truth about the overcrowded conditions, torture, hunger, and frigid weather. Chita, a stop farther ahead, was the most notorious place of exile, with dilapidated wooden houses and dirty unpaved streets where cattle and stray dogs wandered with little consequence. *All too much for a child to understand or even some adults.*

THE TRAIN LEFT Tayshet, heading for the next stop, Irkutsk, then onto Ulan-Ude. The sun was at its highest as they paralleled Lake Baikal. The brilliant sun made the lake's surface sparkle like blue sapphires. Stratus clouds hugged the horizon. The surrounding vegetation varied from chartreuse to emerald green.

"I wish we could stop for a swim," Anya said.

The train came to an unexpected, screeching halt.

"The gods must have heard you," Kira laughed.

Roman lowered the window and stuck his head out. He saw a man waving a white rag. Roman thought about the last time he was on this line when his brother robbed the train. A knock came on the door.

"We will be here for a bit if you wish to stretch your legs," the attendant said.

"What is the problem?" Roman said.

"Some of the tracks are out of alignment. If you wish, I can have the cook pack you a lunch, and you can take it to the lake."

THE THREE AMBLED down the steep embankment to a small sandy beach. Roman and Kira laid out a fleece blanket while Anya headed for the water. She removed her shoes and socks and waded in ankle-deep. "It's not unlike the pond back at the farm. Too cold for swimming."

"Anya, come have some bread and cheese." Kira sat, stretched her legs, and lifted her face to the sun. "It's nice to have the sun on us. I feel like we've been trapped in a miner's cave."

"We will be in Vladivostok within a few days," Roman said.

"I'm nervous. I mean, what can we expect from the people? You, being in the military. Will they be hostile?"

"It's been a military outpost for fifty years. We won't confront the same violence that we did in St. Petersburg. Most citizens are from foreign countries who have major investments in trade."

"I'm excited to go to school and make friends," Anya said.

The whistle blew. Lunch was packed up, and they hiked back to the train.

THE NEXT SEVERAL days were uneventful as the train passed Ulan-Ude and Chita. However, as it rolled into Vladivostok, everyone was filled with anticipation. The station was next to a harbor filled with merchant and military vessels. Kira took Anya's hand as they left the train and walked under the building's iron-roofed canopy.

The streets were littered with vendor's carts pulled by horses and oxen as working electrical wires dangled overhead. Japanese, Chinese, and Europeans dodged trams and motorcars as they crossed busy streets. Roman hailed a carriage. They traveled under an arch. "Anya, this the same arch that the Tsar once rode through," Roman said. They continued through the city of wooden and stone homes, each a marvel. The carriage stopped in front of a two-story rose-colored house.

"Are we home, Mother?"

"Yes, dear."

TWENTY-SEVEN
1911

The Pavlovitch family, weary from their long journey, were brimming with anticipation and hope at the prospect of a fresh start. They exited the hired carriage as the front door to their new home opened. A stocky man dressed in a brown military uniform stood on the single-step stoop.

He saluted Roman. "Major Pavlovitch, I am Lieutenant Ivanov, your aide."

Roman returned his salute and smiled. The lieutenant's name reminded him of his horse. "Allow me to introduce my wife, Mrs. Pavlovitch and my daughter Anya."

The lieutenant bowed. "My pleasure ladies. Let's get you all inside and I'll show you around."

They entered a hallway with diamond-shaped parquet flooring and mustard-yellow painted walls. A long, multicolored, oriental runner ran the length of the hall. To the left was a striking parlor, to the right was a formal dining area, and ahead was a curved staircase that led to the upper floor. At the end of the hallway stood a petite, slender woman with her head lowered. She was dressed in a long blue robe with a wide sash.

"Mother," Anya whispered. "Who is that woman and what is she wearing?"

"A Kimono," Lieutenant Ivanov said. "It's a traditional Japanese garment. She is your servant. I thought you might like to rest and have tea." He ushered them into the parlor without introducing the woman.

Kira's eyes widened to see that their furniture had arrived and been set up. "I'm so happy all of our belongings arrived from St. Petersburg. Thank you for arranging this for us."

The servant poured the tea, set cakes on the mahogany serving table, and left the room. Polite conversation danced around as they sipped tea and nibbled on cake.

"I can't wait to see my bedroom." Anya wiggled in her seat.

Kira laid her hand on Anya's leg to quell her movement. "Patience, dear. Finish your tea."

"Mizuki." Ivanov called for the servant.

Mizuki shuffled into the room.

"Mizuki, show Mrs. Pavlovitch and the girl upstairs. Please excuse us, Mrs. Pavlovitch. I need to speak to your husband." The lieutenant stood up as the three left, then returned to his seat.

"I understand that you were at Port Arthur," Ivanov said.

"Yes. Terrible disappointment. We lost what amounted to the entire fleet."

"I'm happy to report that it has been rebuilt and is stronger than ever here in Vladivostok."

Roman questioned the validity of his report.

Ivanov folded his fingers and set his hands on his lap. "I want to update you on the situation. We have every international industry and its consulates here. They all help to keep the political atmosphere on an even keel. That being said, we do have underlying anarchists that wish to do damage. Certain Chinese factions want the territory restored. The Japanese believe they have territorial rights and use brothels as fronts for espionage operations. Along with us, the French, Dutch, English, and Americans control the banks. Chinese and Koreans make up the majority of the unskilled labor force on the railroad and docks and supply virtually all of the city's produce."

"Then it's what amounts to a political balancing act?"

Ivanov nodded. "And it will be your job to see that things remain stable."

"I understand Kolchak is in town. I'd like to meet with him before he launches his expedition to the Siberian Seas."

"He's at the Versailles Hotel. I'll make lunch arrangements for the two of you."

Anya raced into the room and into her father's arms. "My room looks just like it did back home only bigger."

Roman lifted her on his lap.

"Papa, Mizuki said there are Chinese bandits. Very bad people." Anya bit her lower lip.

"Not to worry, dear." Roman kissed the top of her head and gave Kira a pensive look.

Ivanov stood. "I will leave you for now and pick you up in the morning."

After the lieutenant left the room, Roman said. "Please have a conversation with the servant and tell her not to fill Anya's head with stories."

"I think there's a cultural conflict between the Chinese and Japanese."

"Nevertheless, I don't want that kind of talk in my house."

ROMAN SAT IN the backseat of the black sedan as Lieutenant Ivanov traversed the backside of the mountainous terrain. They reached the top of the hill in front of an enormous concrete fortress. Most of the vegetation at the summit, albeit a few tall trees, had been cleared to provide a clear view of the harbor.

Ivanov stopped the vehicle and pulled on the hand brake. He stepped out and opened the passenger door. "Please follow me, Major."

Ivanov led Roman around several workers on scaffolding. They entered a tunnel that appeared to stretch for miles. A musky odor of damp earth filled Roman's nose. At one point, they passed a room with a massive switchboard encompassing the length of the room. Roman entered a large room to find men sitting behind desks. The room was alive with the jingle-dinging sound of typewriters. Telegraph and telephone lines zigzagged across the ceiling. A massive map of the area filled one wall. A man of average height with a long white mustache and receding white hairline stood reading a memo. He looked up.

Roman approached, clicked his heels, and bowed. "Colonel Orlov, I am Major Pavlovitch."

"Excuse the mess but we are undergoing major reconstruction to fortify the thickness of the walls." The Colonel put the memo down, walked around, and leaned against the desk. "Once the engineers have completed the construction we will have the finest stronghold in the Far East. We will have fifty shore batteries able to withstand the most powerful enemy ships, sixteen forts, and several land batteries." He stood erect with his hands clasped behind him and paced. "I manage a disciplined post. This place is a tinderbox. Your orders are simple. Destroy any building where there's a shot or someone has thrown a bomb. We cannot afford discord."

"Yes, sir," Roman said.

"Good. Glad we understand each other. The

lieutenant will show you to your office."

Roman was used to the callous nature of high-ranking officers. *I'm not sure I've transferred to a better situation. But as long as my family is safe, I shall endure.*

ROMAN RECLINED IN his favorite raggedy overstuffed chair, reading the Vedomosti newspaper from St. Petersburg. Although months behind, he wanted to keep up with the events happening in the West. He turned the page with a loud rattle and sighed in disgust.

Kira turned from the parlor window where she had been admiring the panoramic view of the ships in the harbor. "What the news, dear?"

"It appears we may be heading for another war. The Tsar is advancing further into Persia. Minister Stolypin was gunned down in Kyiv. I'll bet that's a result of the '05 revolt.'"

"Masha said they are exporting grain while the peasants starve." Kira wrung her hands. "They must need money."

"It seems there's some upheaval about a monk's involvement with the Imperial family."

"Remember, I told you about how creepy he was when we were in Crimea."

Roman nodded.

"I don't wish to hear about things back home anymore. It's too upsetting."

"We must keep abreast in case we need to take action."

Kira sighed and returned to the window.

Roman turned to the next page. "Oh my. Leo Tolstoy died. I served with his son Andre at Port Arthur. I will write him a condolence letter."

Roman set aside the paper and approached Kira. From behind, he encircled his arms around her waist, feeling the warmth of her body. "Are you happy we moved?"

She leaned into his body and sighed. "As long as we are together, I am happy."

TWENTY-EIGHT

1911-1912

KIRA STRAIGHTENED HERSELF and cleared her throat. "Roman, I plan to go to the department store later today to pick up a few things. I also plan to get theater tickets. Isadora Duncan is going to perform at the Pushkin Theater later this month. I want to see what all the fuss is regarding her dance style."

Roman smiled at his wife, knowing there was no recourse in objecting. He reached for a piece of breakfast toast. Before he could take a bite, a violent boom vibrated through the house. The sound wave's energy caused a single glass pane to crack and paintings to shift catawampus. Everyone sat wide-eyed and held their breaths for a moment. Kira clutched her chest. Anya cried out and scrambled into her mother's arms. Mizuki scurried into the room from the kitchen. The swinging door caught her from behind, and she bounced two steps forward. Roman raced to the picture window to see a black plume of smoke fill the harbor sky.

"What happened, Papa?" The trace of a tremor resonated in Anya's voice.

"An accident—I hope." Roman rushed to grab his hat and coat. As he approached the door, he turned to Kira. "You had better postpone your shopping for another day."

SOLDIERS PILED INTO transportation trucks as Roman walked into the military fortress. He had come from the docks where he had investigated the explosion.

"Colonel Orlov," he saluted. "I'm sorry to report that today's incident has destroyed building materials stacked on the dock."

"What was the cause?"

"Unknown at this time."

"How much can be recovered?"

"About a third."

"Son-of-a-bitch." Orlov rose from his seat, tugged on his blue double-breasted tunic, and cleared his throat. "I just received word that a revolution uprising has occurred in southern China. The revolutionaries have forced the emperor and royal family to abdicate the throne. There is a power struggle throughout China. Chinese warlords are taking territorial control, probably led by the *Kokuryūkai, a* Japanese society trained in espionage. They are probably siding with their mortal enemy to force us and the Europeans out of China." Orlov paced the room.

Roman pondered his reason for leaving Russia for the Far East. *I guess there is no escaping violence in today's world.*

"I know this is the work of the Japanese. I can smell it. I want you to raid the most popular Japanese brothel and imprison everyone in the joint. We will hit them in their pocketbook."

"Won't that upset the Europeans?"

"I can't be concerned with their depravity. We need to contain this terrorism before it escalates."

ROMAN ENTERED THE *Sakura* brothel and was met by several almond-eyed women peering from powder-white faces and mouths reminiscent of crimson gashes. Their black hair was tied back in tight buns at the back of the neck with wing-like extensions on either side of the head. They wore kimonos from varying colors of the spectrum. The odor of cigarette smoke fused with a humid sweetness circulated in the air.

Roman waved his men forward. The soldiers, with roughness, corralled screaming women. One woman tried to scratch a soldier's face. He forcefully knocked her to the floor with the butt of his gun. Soldiers marched up the stairs, entered occupied rooms, and emptied them. Footsteps echoed through the halls and down the steps. Scantily clad women and shirtless men buttoned their trousers while spewing profanities.

Roman understood their English and French scorn.

"Let the Europeans and Americans go. Round up the others, place them in the wagon, and take them to the prison." Roman recounted the Colonel's harsh words of wanting the place decimated. He allowed the men to bust things up but refused to burn the building to the ground. *No good will come from it.*

KIRA REFUSED TO heed Roman's words and found herself at the center of town. The fire had been extinguished, but lingering smoke encompassed the air. People held handkerchiefs over their faces as they continued on their way. She had taken Anya with her but now regretted her decision. A young Chinese man approached. Kira held her breath and skirted Anya behind her, remembering Mizuki's words about Chinese bandits. The man tipped his hat and passed them without incident. Kira exhaled, feeling a bit foolish but also a wave of relief. She took Anya's hand and entered the three-story department store.

"May I help you, madam?" A clerk said.

"No, thank you." Kira preferred to browse at her own speed. Thumbing through various colored linens, she lost sight of Anya. Kira called out, but no response. Her heart and mind started to race. She ran up and down the aisles, calling out. Still no response. Beads of sweat began to form along her hairline.

The clerk approached. "Is something wrong?"

"I can't find my daughter."

The clerk smiled. "Come with me."

There, sitting on a three-legged stool reading a book, was Anya.

Kira ran to her daughter, picked her up, hugged and kissed her, then slapped her face. Kira's hand shook. She had never struck her daughter before. She knew it had been an automatic reflex and felt her stomach twist.

Anya's eyes opened as wide as a gold ruble. She touched her tear-drenched cheeks.

"Don't you ever leave my side when we are out, do you understand?"

Still rubbing her red cheek, Anya nodded.

"Let's not tell Papa. This will be our little secret." Kira took her daughter to her breast and held her tight until Anya struggled to catch a breath.

Not deterred from the excitement, Kira still achieve her goal of purchasing theatre tickets.

TWENTY-NINE
1912-1913

Anya bounded into the dining room. "Ohayō, Papa. Kyō wa genkidesu ka?"

Roman looked up from the morning newspaper with a quizzical expression.

"Mizuki is teaching me Japanese." Anya stood with her hands on her hips. "I asked, how you are this morning."

"I'm fine. Thank you." He took a sip of coffee and returned to his paper.

Kira entered the room and proceeded to spoon buckwheat porridge into a bowl from the sideboard, and sat at the table.

"The paper reports that Austria has claimed Bosnian territory," Roman said. "The Serbs are up in arms. If they're not careful there will be war."

Kira pushed her porridge around with a spoon. She

sat up in her chair and cleared her throat. "Mizuki told us she and her sister came to Vladivostok due to the famine in Japan."

"Is her sister a servant too?" Roman turned to the next page.

A sneeze erupted from behind a cracked in the open kitchen door.

Kira shifted her eyes and responded in a monotone voice. "She is in a brothel. Mizuki said her sister tried to get her name removed from the list of prostitutes but they would only accept it if the owner of the brothel countersigned. He refuses. She tried to enlist the American Salvation Army but ruffians beat the soldier who tried to help." Kira shifted in her chair. "Do you think there is anything you might do so she can obtain respectable work?"

Roman ruffled his paper. "Kira, I don't have any authority over these matters." He looked at Kira's downturned lips and sighed. "I'll see what I can do."

Kira caressed his hand and kissed it. "Thank you."

The kitchen door swung shut.

ROMAN ENTERED THE command room to see Colonel Orlov reading a telegraph. A scowl consumed Orlov's face. "Some damn lawyer wrote about a massacre at the Lena River. Seems there were over 250 gold miners killed by a brigade of soldiers." He shook the paper until it fell to the ground. "There have been over 1000 strikes in St Petersburgh alone." Orlov smacked his fist into the palm of the other hand. "It's the intelligentsia that we need to watch. I want you to take a company and break up any social gatherings."

"Do you think that could evoke an insurrection?"

"I will not tolerate any unrest. Is that understood?"

"Yes, sir." Roman saluted his commander and left the room. *I refuse to turn this into another Bloody Sunday … first, I need to do something.*

ROMAN SAT AT a long metal rectangle table in a grey sterile detention room. Across from him sat the owner of the brothel they had raided earlier.

"I am in a position to improve your current situation or make it intolerable," Roman said.

The Japanese man across from him, the size of a sumo wrestler, returned a blank stare.

"Do you understand what I am saying?"

No response.

Roman slammed his hand on the desk. A loud, tinny sound exploded. The man jumped and then nodded.

"Good. I understand you have a woman by the name of Aiko. Sign this document releasing her from any obligations." He slid the paper across the table.

A scowl crossed the man's face. "How does it benefit me?"

Roman smirked. "Freedom from my wrath."

SOLDIERS, WHEN CONFRONTED by antagonists, remained calm per Roman's instruction. He believed his men's presence would dissuade most from assembling. Although, a few did gather at the main square, shouting with raised newspapers overhead. Roman assumed the articles relayed the unrest spreading throughout the country. The soldiers walked the perimeter, guns slung over their shoulders. A few protesters shouted at them. The soldiers turned to face the antagonists from a distance but remained at attention. When one man in a black full-length coat started to approach, a few soldiers went for their rifles.

Roman shouted. "Hold your position."

A friend of the aggressor pulled him away. Several disgruntled men left the square mumbling unrecognizable words.

There was a report of vandalism at a nearby merchant. Roman took a few men to investigate, but by the time they arrived, the street was cleared with no sign of destruction. The soldiers moved on and continued to patrol the city. By nightfall, Roman felt a sense of accomplishment, knowing that any opposition had been avoided, and dismissed his men.

EXHAUSTED FROM THE day's ordeal, Roman flopped into his favorite chair. Kira entered the room and handed him a glass of vodka. She walked over to the secretary and thumbed through envelopes. "I see we received letters from Masha and my mother."

Kira opened the drawer of the neoclassic mahogany secretary and picked up the red enameled letter opener.

She inserted the blade into the top flap of one letter and slid it to the other side. She repeated the process with the second letter. She removed Masha's letter first and sat on the settee.

"Oh my." Kira sighed

"What is it?" Roman said.

"Masha said she had another spell the other day, went to the infirmary, but she is now back home and feeling better." Kira paused. "I think I should go to Moscow."

"I'm sure she is doing all right. I don't want you traveling across the country with all the unrest and the rumor of war on a precipice."

"But I feel she needs me."

Roman took a sip. "Let's see if things settle down in the next few weeks."

Kira opened her mother's letter and started to read. She screamed a shrill Roman had never heard before.

"What's wrong?"

Kira's entire body trembled as the letter fell to the floor. Sobbing, she pointed to the letter.

> My Precious Daughter,
>
> I'm sorry to tell you that your Auntie has passed. She was gravely ill for several months, and her heart simply gave way. She is resting in her husband's family crypt. She refused to let us tell you earlier because she didn't want you to travel in these trying times.
>
> We are all heartbroken with Auntie's passing. She has left you an inheritance.

Your father will set up a wire transfer to the Sberbank in Vladivostok and send a telegram with further instructions. It's imperative that we move on this quickly.

My dearest wish is for the safety of you all.
Your Loving Mother

Roman caressed Kira in his arms and stroked her hair as she wept.

Anya ran into the room. "What happened?"

"Mother received sad news today. I need you to ready yourself for bed. I will be up in a few minutes to say goodnight." Roman gathered up his weeping wife and carried her to their bedroom.

THIRTY

1913

ANYA SAT ON the davenport snuggled next to her father as he read to her. "Papa, when is Mama going to feel better?"

"She misses her Auntie. Give her some time. It's only been a week. Masha was a second mother to her and she's is upset that she wasn't able to visit her one last time."

"I know, but I was hoping to go clothes shopping. I need new tights … and well … I'm afraid to ask because it disturbs me to see her eyes leak and her lips twist."

Roman put down the book and placed his arm around her. "Instead, how about we go to the firing range?"

"Oh, that would be grand." Anya smiled as wide as a melon slice.

"I'll go tell your mother."

Roman's military position allowed him to bring his daughter to the officer's gun range. He handed Anya his Mosin-Nagant rifle. "Let's go through the steps."

"Yes, Papa."

"Place the rifle in your left hand. Let the barrel rest in the "V" created by your thumb and forefinger. The grip should be light and your wrist straight with the fingers curled naturally around the handguard."

"Like this?"

"Make sure the butt is steadied against your shoulder, not the fleshy part of your armpit." Roman had added padding to the butt of the rifle to reduce the impact from the recoil. "Don't curl your finger around the trigger until you're ready to fire. You want to squeeze the trigger as if you were bringing your finger to your fist."

Roman saw his daughter tense up. "Relax your shoulder. That will ease the recoil. Take a deep breath, hold it and squeeze the trigger."

Anya followed her father's instructions and squeezed the trigger. The energy kickback pushed her backward, causing her to gasp and giggle.

Roman looked through the binoculars at the target. A satisfied smile crossed his face. "Nicely done. Almost a bullseye."

"I can do better." Anya shot several more times with a result of 90 percent at or near the center.

"You're a natural, sweetie." He patted her on the back.

"I love to shoot, but I'm not sure I could kill a living animal or, for that matter a person."

"To take another life can be a haunting experience that will stay with you forever. However, if it comes to saving yourself, what you've learned today will assist in your survival. Let's pray you never have to meet that circumstance."

WEEKS HAD PASSED, and Kira's spirits had uplifted somewhat. She was preparing a roast chicken for supper when Anya entered the room after returning from school. "What did you learn today, dear?"

"Apparently, there is a raging epidemic of typhus racing through the country."

"Is that so?" Kira turned from her daughter to squash a smile. She knew what was coming.

"Yes," Anya said, "and I've decided to become a doctor to help cure people." She took a bite of an apple.

"That's nice, dear." Kira listened attentively to her daughter, knowing that next week, she would move on to another career interest. Last week, she had dreamt of becoming a teacher, the week before a ballerina. Kira was glad they had moved to Vladivostok. Many scientists, chemists, and mathematicians who had flooded the city had set up a children's learning center. It opened a world for her daughter that she believed might never have been exposed to in St. Petersburg.

"You need to get ready for ballet practice. And

don't forget your new tights."

"Yes, Mamma." Anya left the room to collect her dance bag. "Hello, Papa," Anya said in passing.

Roman entered the kitchen and gently kissed the nape of Kira's neck.

"Mizuki is visiting her sister and I'm busy here," Kira said. "Can you walk Anya to dance practice?"

"I'm not sure why she needs such a rigorous schedule; dance, schoolwork, even language lessons. She's fluent in French and Russian, with a bit of English, Japanese, and Chinese thrown in. She'll just end up marrying a soldier like myself." He stood tall and smiled.

"I want her prepared for life. You recall it's a new century." She gave him a self-satisfied smirk. "Besides, it builds self-assurance and poise. I also want her to take formal ballroom dancing so she'll be ready for her debut."

"You plan to take her across the Urals?"

"Some day. I want to visit my parents and take Anya with me."

No longer listening, Roman glanced at the newspaper on the table. The headlines read, "Russia Commemorates the Tercentenary of Romanov Rule." Underneath in smaller type, "US Swears in 28th President, Woodrow Wilson." Below was a picture of a man strapped into a straightjacket suspended by his ankles from a tall building. Under the photo, it read, "Escape Artist Houdini Defies Gravity." Roman shook his head. "Americans."

Anya walked into the room. "I'm ready."

"It might rain, so you'll need your galoshes and coat," Kira said. "Roman, on your way home, will you stop by the grocer and pick up bread and butter?"

"Yes, dear." He kissed his wife, and he and Anya left.

ROMAN AND ANYA walked toward the dance studio. A light rain sprinkled their faces—not enough for an umbrella but just enough to be annoying. Anya giggled as she stomped in a puddle from a previous downpour.

"Anya, how do you feel about all your studies and outside classes? Do you think it's too much?"

"I enjoy being with my friends. My teachers are very nice and I learn lots of new things."

"What about all the dance classes?"

"It's okay. Mother says it gives me an advantage for my future. I don't care one way or the other, but I don't want to disappoint her."

"If it becomes too burdensome let me know … okay?"

"Yes, Papa."

THIRTY-ONE
1914

1914 BEGAN AS a year of prosperity for the Pavlovitch family. Unfortunately, by summer, the world turned unreceptive to reason. Vladivostok had become an international scientific, cultural, and industrial center. Sadly, it also brought in a criminal element. The streets overran with various countries' militaries, all under the guise of protecting their interests. Within their close-knit community, a sense of peace remained despite the chaos that reigned outside their periphery.

Despite all the strife, Roman felt assured that he had made the right decision to relocate the family. He sat at the kitchen table, savoring his morning coffee. He picked up the newspaper to read the headline: GERMANY DECLARES WAR ON RUSSIA.

"Oh, my god," he shouted.

Kira jumped, spilling milk on the table.

"Mother, you missed my porridge bowl," Anya said.

Kira fetched a rag to wipe up the spill. "What is it, dear?"

"War. I told you when the Austrian Archduke was assassinated in Serbia, things would escalate. You know all this land grab with Africa and the Slavic nations have created an intolerable situation. I fear we may not be prepared."

Kira remained quiet, knowing her words would do nothing to erase his fears as well as her own.

Anya said, "Papa, if the Tsar and Kaiser are related, why, are they going to war against each other?"

"It's a tangled web of loyalties. Russia has an alliance with Serbia, and Germany has an alliance with Austria-Hungary."

"It seems irrational," Anya said.

"Yes, in some ways it is." Roman continued to read the article. "The good news is there's a patriotic union in Russia amongst the country causing a downturn in the strikes."

"I hope war won't come here," Kira said

"I might transfer our currency to another country as a precaution.

"I wonder what this means for the boys back home?"

"Yes, I wonder." Roman rubbed his chin. "I'll write to Uri today."

WEEKS LATER, ROMAN received a letter from Uri. He read it to Kira.

"Roman,

So good to hear from you, my dear friend. First, the good news. My wife gave birth to a beautiful baby boy. We named him Pyotr. A name that holds great significance to our family history. I now understand your fierce passion for protecting your family.

You are fortunate to be far from here. There is considerable fear and anxiety, not only among the peasantry but also within the highest echelons. Germany declared war on France and Britain. They are morally obligated to fight with us. We hope to squeeze the Huns into submission within the year. God knows when the Americans will join us, but they have promised supplies. Your station will play a crucial role in this war effort.

Fëdor was transferred to the front—the poor devil. He witnessed a fistfight between two generals. As you know, most of these aristocrats couldn't fight themselves out of a sack of potatoes.

I received a promotion to your old post and rank. Boris is not pleased that he was passed over. I thought for sure his uncle would intervene. Instead, they gave him command of an infantry unit to maintain order in the streets. God, save us.

You may already know that Kolchak commands the Baltic Fleet. Reports say things are going so well that he may be up for a very high promotion.

I hope we shall see each other soon.
Your humble friend,
Uri."

Roman put the letter down. "I'm happy for Uri's addition to his family. And equally pleased for his promotion. I pray Fëdor remains safe. Uri's assessment of Boris's assignment is right. He is too quick-tempered and arrogant to avoid an escalation from any confrontation."

BY LATE FALL, the war was in full swing. St. Petersburg was renamed Petrograd to sound more Russian rather than Germanic. As Uri had predicted, Vladivostok became the chief Pacific entry port for military supplies and railway equipment from the United States. Pushing supplies to the Russian front made Roman's days long. Adding to the difficulty was the incompletion of the Siberian Railroad to Vladivostok. A diverse workforce, including Chinese labor, was brought in to complete the railway.

Each day, more people arrived in the city. Food had been diverted to the war effort, leading to shortages, creating homelessness and starvation throughout the western part of the country. Unlike in some nations, where bread was supplemented with dried potatoes, oats, barley, or even straw, that was not the case in the East. Crops continued to grow and be harvested, although meat, coffee, tea, and sugar were in short supply.

Roman lumbered into the apartment from working late that night. He fell into his favorite overstuffed chair and threw his feet onto the hassock.

"How was your day?" Kira handed him a vodka.

"Horrific. Constant demands to get supplies expediently to the front … that damn railway needs to be completed." He sighed. "I'm hoping it's done before the end of the year." He sipped his drink and rested his head on the back of the chair.

Kira went into the kitchen and returned with a drink refill. Even with shortages, they were still able to acquire some comforts.

"I received a letter from my mother," Kira said. "The war is at their front door. Several factories have closed their doors, and the army has moved its headquarters to Minsk. My father is forced to stay, but he made plans to have my mother and siblings move to St. Petersburg. I don't know if St. Petersburg or Moscow are any less turbulent." Her stomach twisted as she thought about her sister. "I'm worried about Catherine. She looked so frail the last time I saw her. I feel I should say something to Mother … but I promised not to say anything. I wish they would come here." She paused. "We are very fortunate to be on this side of the war and to have Masha's inheritance."

"Yes, dear." His eyes were closed. Before the drink was about to spill, Kira slowly pried the glass from his fingers. She kissed him on the forehead and left him to sleep.

THIRTY-TWO

1915

WAR CONSUMED THE world. Strikes and riots were rampant in Russian cities. Chaos seemed to be the prevailing law. Russia's claim on Constantinople allowed its naval ships to easily pass from the Black Sea to open waters, further infuriating the Germans.

Roman sat at the kitchen table reading the morning newspaper. He released a heavy exhale.

Kira placed a lock of fallen hair behind her ear and poured herself a cup of coffee. "What is it, dear?"

"The Germans have torpedoed the Italian liner, *Ancona* on its way to New York."

"Didn't they sink a British ocean liner earlier this year after pledging to the world the waters were safe?"

"You can't trust those Huns. There were many losses on both ships. Seems the Americans have finally turned against the Germans. They'll be in the war soon."

"I hope this conflict ends soon." Kira sighed.

"I've hesitated to tell you something." He paused and put down the newspaper. "Things are not going well at the front. The word is that they may recruit retired officers and relocate officers posted in outlying areas."

Kira froze with the cup at her lips. "Does that mean you?"

"It's possible."

"Oh, Roman, I don't think I can stand to have you leave again. What about your shortness of breath? They can't expect you to fight."

Roman patted Kira's hand. "Let's not dwell on it until we hear something."

"Dwell on what?" Anya said as she walked into the room with a book.

Roman ignored her question. "What are you reading?"

"Mizuki gave it to me to practice my Japanese. Its *The Secret Garden* translated. I'd want to travel to England and see this garden."

"I don't believe it's a real place, dear. It's only a story," Kira said.

"Oh, it's real all right."

Kira and Roman looked at each other with reluctant smiles. Roman rose from his seat. "I'll be off to work. What have you planned for the day?"

"Several church ladies are assembling food parcels for the boys at the front. We hand them over to the

Political Red Cross who send them on."

Anya piped up, "I want to help."

"You can stop by after school."

IT WASN'T MORE than a few weeks before Roman received a letter from the military ordering his return to Petrograd for reassignment. Given the geographical distance, he considered ignoring the letter, but his strong sense of duty disallowed him to capitulate. *A coward flees. A man of duty accepts his fate.* He immediately sent a letter to Uri, who responded.

> Roman,
>
> Good to hear from you, my old friend. You are right. Things are not going as expected on the front or here at home. There is great unrest with food shortages. People are starving in the streets. The government's lack of efforts to defuse the crisis and all the different factions attempting to impose their non-Christian social reform have plunged the country into turmoil. The stench in the air is stifling, and the need for action is pressing.
>
> You may have yet to hear about Alekander Samsonov, whom you were with at the Battle of Mukden. He failed to advance the cavalry through German lines at Tannenberg. The disgrace of his failure was too much for him to bear—he committed suicide.
>
> To avoid the front, I strongly recommend you reach out to Kolchak. See if he can transfer you to his company in the Black Sea.
>
> Your Dear Friend,
>
> Uri

ROMAN ARRIVED IN Petrograd. Saying goodbye to his family had been filled with hugs and kisses and fraught with sadness. He felt the pain of anguish, having defaulted on his promise never to leave them.

After the long trip a wave of relief washing over him once he saw Uri waiting for him at the train station.

"It's so good to see you, my old friend," Uri said as he embraced Roman, kissing him on both cheeks.

"You look good in your commander's uniform," Roman said.

"Let's get something to eat and catch up."

They entered a tavern secluded down an alleyway. The smoke-filled room was dank. Several old timers sat huddled in the corner. Uri shouted at the barkeep for drinks as they sat.

"What news have you from the front?" Roman said.

"Nothing has changed since I last wrote you. I heard from Fëdor." Uri shook his head. "The fool volunteered for the front to improve his rank."

Roman chuckled. "I can see him chewing on his mustache, gripping a rifle."

Uri laughed a bit, then stopped. "He's in the trenches and says they're brutal. Miles long filled with rainwater, corpses, and endless grey days. They have no way to send the dead home for a proper burial without being gun fodder themselves so they walk on their graves. The Germans are using chemicals. A type of gas that causes skin rash, trouble breathing, and vomiting. It's quite terrible. Oh, before I forget. You remember Kira's old beau, Colonel Vershinin." Uri snickered. "He finally succumbed to his disease. According to gossip it was several days before they found his bloated-body floating in the river. No one knows how he got there but one might assume?"

Roman had no response to the news. "What of Boris?"

"In typical Boris fashion, he's causing trouble. He can't allow the protesters to march peacefully along the streets without bayonetting one or two, which creates more insurrectionists."

"He better be careful, or one day that bayonet may be his comeuppance."

Uri filled his glass and downed it. "I'm not sure we should have ended serfdom." His words started to slur. "It's provided the peasants more freedom to organize."

"Having once been a farmer and lived among them, it's a hard life. Most of your earnings go to taxes, leaving little to put on the table."

"I know, but all these machine factories in the city have caused overcrowding and poor living conditions." He raised his arms to the ceiling and shouted. "This was once the most beautiful city."

"Lower your voice, Uri."

"These old men don't care what we say." He downed another shot. "Most of them probably agree."

"We had to obtain industry to keep up with other nations. I read the *Figaro* newspaper. It gives me insight into what the world has to say. The world thinks Russia is an impoverished and backward nation."

"The only thing we read in the newspaper is how great things are going. But with my own eyes, I have seen the number of returning dead and casualties that pass through the streets. If this war does not end soon there will surely be a revolution." Uri ran his hands through his hair. "These Bolsheviks may have it right. A substantial majority of people," he whispered, "even some soldiers have joined their cause. They have lost confidence in the Tsar's leadership."

"I understand, but I can't believe equalized labor is the answer. It means someone is still at the top leaving corruption to abound."

Uri's eyes closed, and his chin sunk to his chest.

"Let's get out of here." Roman helped Uri out of his seat.

ROMAN DECIDED TO seek out his brother. It took some time, but through Uri's help, he found him holed up in an abandoned warehouse with a band of renegades.

"I can't believe you are here." Artie grabbed Roman with a forceful hug and kissed him on both cheeks. "Is the family with you?"

"Not this time. I'm here for reassignment."

"You deserted your beautiful wife and child?"

"I did not …" He paused and slumped. "I had no choice."

"Brother, there is always a choice."

Roman looked around at the makeshift living area, paper peeling off the walls, and the floor looked like it had not been swept in years. Ratty mattresses lay haphazardly. Non-functioning electrical wires dangled loosely from the ceiling like lifeless snakes. The most egregious smell of human waste and sweat permeated the area. "I see you've done well for yourself."

"We are in transition. In case you haven't heard— the people are taking over."

Roman felt his face flush and his hands clench. As children, Artie always had a way of getting him riled. Or, maybe it was Artie's way to try and get him to see things in a different light. Roman wasn't sure, but at that moment, he didn't care. "Artie … you can't tell me these things."

"Let's get out of here and have a drink some- where," Artie suggested.

THIRTY-THREE

1915-1916

Kira and Anya sat quietly at the kitchen table. Roman's absence had left an emptiness in the home and their hearts.

"How about I make some breakfast?" Kira said.

"Oh, Mama, I'm not hungry."

"I know, but you need to eat. Papa will be home soon. We need to carry on the way he asked us." She leaned over and stroked Anya's head. "How about if I read your father's letter?"

Anya let out a long sigh. "Alright."

> My Dear Loved Ones,
>
> I miss you so very much. I hope this letter finds you well. I feel very fortunate to be stationed in Sevastopol. Kira, you remember what a lovely time we had those many years ago.

"It's where we discovered I was with child—you." Kira bopped Anya's nose

Anya giggled.

Kira smiled and continued reading.

> "I am serving with the Black Fleet. I'm more of a horseman, but I find solace in my shipmates and the beauty of the sea.
>
> While in Petrograd, I visited your mother and sisters. Your sister Catherine lay sick in bed. Your mother believes she will be well soon, and you should not worry."

Kira stopped reading. Her stomach twisted. She felt her face flush.

"Are you all right, Mother??

"I'm worried about my sister." She continued reading.

> "Your father is still in Minsk but plans to join the family soon. I met with Artie. He's in deep with the anarchists. They believe we should not have entered into this war. They deem it an imperialist war. They might be right. The army has suffered unbelievable losses. How can the government expect to maintain rule without an army? I worry for the future. I am relieved that you are far from the chaos and safe."

"We are too," Anya said, "but we miss you."

"We do indeed. He sends his love and asks that you keep up your schoolwork."

"Where does it say that?"

"I'm relaying what Papa forgot to say."

Anya gave her a mock salute.

"Now, how about some breakfast?"

"Yes, please."

THAT EVENING, AS Anya slept, Kira sat down to respond to Roman's letter.

> My Darling,
>
> It warms my heart to hear from you. We are all doing well here. Thousands of Chinese are being shipped to Britain, France, and Russia to fill the labor shortage. They will repair tanks, assemble shells, and transport supplies and munitions. I hope these efforts contribute to ending this war.
>
> The railway from Khabarovsk to Vladivostok has been completed, a significant benefit. I know you are not here to discuss it, but I have decided to visit my family in Petrograd. My mother tells me that Grand Duchess Maria is having her cotillion. I plan to take Anya, as they had been playmates. It will also be an excellent opportunity to introduce her to society.
>
> It saddens me to give you unfavorable news, but Anya has been difficult since you left. She has been moping around and misbehaving. She misses you.
>
> We will be arriving in St. Petersburg within a month. See if you can join us even for a few days to lighten her spirits.
>
> All my love,
> Kira

KIRA AND ANYA arrived in Petrograd later that month. Kira's mother and two of her three sisters met them at the station.

"Where is Catherine?" Kira said.

"She's a bit peaked but anxiously waiting for you to arrive. She's engaged now and eagerly anticipating the wedding."

"She wrote me and spoke very highly of him."

"I'm not sure when we will ever get the other two married." Her mother sighed and climbed into the waiting cab. Her sisters rolled their eyes and followed their mother.

"Is father here?"

"He hopes to join us within a few weeks. How was your journey?"

"Long. Some parts were beautiful, others not so much. Anya remembered a few areas from the time we moved back east."

"I see you're no longer wearing a corset." Kira's mother pursed her lips and raised an eyebrow of disapproval.

"Mother, the government has asked us not to buy corsets so they can use the metal to build ships?"

"You don't have an old one?"

Kira refused to argue further.

"You'll need to borrow one from Catherine if you plan to attend the cotillion."

"Yes, Mother." Kira stared out the window as they passed through the streets.

"I have arranged for a dressmaker to fit Anya for a gown."

Anya clapped her hands and bounced in her seat.

"Dear," Kira said, "please be still. A lady does not bounce."

Anya smiled at her grandmother with gratitude.

They arrived at a blue and white trimmed Empire-style house in time for tea and *syrniki*. Kira immediately went up to Catherine's room to check on her. She entered the bedroom to find Catherine sitting upright in a canopy bed. A mauve-colored flower print quilt lay across her. A geometric lavender paper covered the walls. Kira's heart ached at the sight of Catherine's pale face. Her once billowy pink cheeks were sunken and colorless.

"How are you feeling?" Kira leaned in to kiss her on both cheeks, then sat on a gothic revival chair next to the bed. Catherine's illness had been a mystery to the family, and the doctor's lack of a precise diagnosis did little to comfort anyone.

"Better now that you are here. The doctor gave me these pills." She pointed to them on the nightstand. "He said I should be better in a few days.

Kira picked up the bottle. Her heart sank as she read the word laudanum. She was well versed in the terrible addiction that came with the overuse of this narcotic.

"Sister, you be careful with these."

"I'm anxious for you to meet my fiancé, but he is

serving at the Austrian border. He's a military man like Roman. He is tall and very handsome."

"Is he good to you?"

"Yes. He is a very gentle and kind man." Catherine became short of breath and slumped back under the covers. "I'm quite tired. I think I'll sleep for a bit and try to come down for supper."

"I'll come back later and check on you." Kira walked out the door.

Catherine did not join everyone for supper. Several days passed before she found the energy to dress and join the family. Kira was deeply disturbed by Catherine's grey complexion.

KIRA, ANYA, AND the rest of the family, excluding Catherine, entered the palace ballroom. The high curved ceiling, adorned with a different religious mural in each panel. Three crystal chandeliers provided ambient light. Round tables filled the room. Each table was covered with silver candlesticks, painted dinnerware, and floral arrangements.

Anya had her auburn hair pulled back with curls cascaded down her back. Her cream dress fell just below the knee. The bodice had several rows of vertical ruffles. A three-inch sash, tied at the hipline and finished with a red accent bow, presented a perfect accent. Below the sash were two layers of ruffles. Her hands were shielded by white gloves.

Kira fidgeted with her borrowed corset. Her

mother frowned at her daughter's lack of decorum. Kira turned her head away from her disapproving face. She noticed her wide-eyed daughter taking in all the glamor and brilliant surroundings. When Anya spotted the Grand Duchess Maria, Kira held her back from running to embrace her. "Not now, dear."

Maria stood out in a pink gown and jeweled tiara that graced her head. Her upturned dark blue eyes darted around the room as she admired the young officers. Men not in uniform wore black double-breasted frock coats, light grey waistcoats, Ascot-knotted cravats, light gloves, and dress boots. Several elderly women wore out-of-fashion bustles.

The Majesties, Grand Dukes, and their wives were seated at the center table. Guests with varying statuses sat at various surrounding tables, each placement a subtle indicator of their standing in the royal court. Kira's family found their place cards at the farthest point from the center. The regimental band played music during dinner. Small dishes with a variety of meats, flatbread, vegetables, and desserts were served throughout the evening. Being Anya's first royal formal dinner, Kira helped her with the tableware.

After dinner, everyone lined up to be presented to the Imperial family. During that time, the tables were taken away to prepare the room for dancing. After the procession, the Tsar called over the regimental commander and presented him to Maria. She batted her eyes as her face turned red when he kissed her gloved hand. He led her onto the dance floor, where they danced alone for several minutes before others joined.

"Mother, Maria barely acknowledged me," Anya said.

"This is her night, dear. She has put away her playthings and childhood friends. She is now a young woman and will soon marry." Anya's only reaction was to wrinkle her nose.

Kira circulated the room and reminisced with old acquaintances. At one point, she spotted Anya speaking with several other girls. However, by midnight, Anya was slumped in a chair asleep. With the Tsar in another room playing cards and the Tsarina preoccupied, Kira took the opportunity to slip away and take Anya back to the house.

As they climbed the stairs to the front door, it suddenly opened. Kira stopped in her tracks.

Anya yelled, "Papa."

THIRTY-FOUR

1916-1917

KIRA EMBRACED ROMAN and wiped her joyous tears on his chest. Anya sandwiched herself between her parents. She squeezed him so hard Roman had to loosen her grip to catch his breath.

"Anya, remember that your papa has issues breathing," Kira said.

"I know, but I missed him so."

"How long are you with us?" Kira said.

"A short time, my love." He held her head and kissed her mouth.

Anya turned red. "Oh, Papa." Kira and Roman laughed.

"Are you hungry?" Kira said.

Roman nodded.

"Let's see what we can muster up." Kira found leftover cutlets and some cheeses in the icebox. Roman opened a bottle of wine as they sat in the kitchen.

"Papa, did you see my beautiful dress that Babka made for me?" Anya twirled as the dress flowed gracefully around her.

"You look lovely." He drew her close to his side and kissed her cheek. "It's good to be together."

Anya raced out of the room shouting. "I want to show you something."

While Anya was out of the room, Roman whispered to Kira. "I've made arrangements to go to Fabergé's studio while I'm here to have a ring designed for Anya's sixteenth birthday."

"But that won't be for a few more years."

"I know, but who knows when either of us will be back in the area again."

Anya reentered the room. "What are you two whispering about?"

"Your mother tells me you two plan to see *The Sleeping Beauty* tomorrow.

Anya's eyes widened. "Oh, mother. I so wanted to see it. I am so happy." She wrapped her arms around Kira's neck and hugged her.

"What are you carrying?" Roman said.

Anya laid a loop of black onyx beads on the table. "They're prayer beads, used to recite the Jesus prayer. Babka is teaching me."

"These days we need all the prayers we can marshal," Roman said.

ROMAN SLIPPED OUT of the house the next day while Kira and Anya readied themselves for the Matinee.

He was stunned by the mingling of red and fuchsia splashes of streaks illuminating the morning sky.

Several steps from his destination, Roman was confronted by a crowd of people, including women and children, holding signs protesting their working conditions and a lack of food. They marched in the middle of the street, impeding traffic. Their gaunt faces and clothes that hung loosely on their boney frames. A flash of guilt filled Roman, having finished a hardy breakfast earlier. To avoid possible hostility, Roman quickly turned the corner and found himself at his destination.

His heels clicked on the polished red granite as he entered the Art Nouveau building with its neo-Gothic elements. Sunlight poured in through various stained glass windows, casting a rainbow of colors along a wide staircase. At the end of the room sat a man behind a Louis XV walnut desk. The man rose to greet him. He was slight in stature, with a white beard and a hairline that receded to the crown.

"Welcome to the house of Fabergé. You are here to have a ring designed for your daughter?"

"Yes, sir," Roman said.

"Please, have a seat." He directed Roman to an Empire Period chair.

"Tell me what you have in mind and my craftsmen will create a most elegant design."

"I don't have a precise idea. However, I need the gems to represent white for liberty, blue for loyalty, and red for courage. It must be fitting for a young woman."

The jeweler nodded. "Most excellent."

"Let me know the amount and I'll have my bank transfer the money. My wife will pick it up. You can reach her at this number." Roman handed the man a card.

THE FAMILY SAT around the dining table as servants provided roasted lamb and cabbage for the evening meal. Catherine sat across from Roman. Looking at her, his thoughts returned to the gaunt faces in the streets he witnessed earlier.

Roman turned his attention to his daughter. "Anya, did you enjoy the ballet?"

"The princess was beautiful as she fluttered around in the enchanted forest. And the prince was very handsome." Anya's brows furrowed. "The fairy was very wicked." Laughter engulfed everyone.

A forceful knock at the front door shattered the tranquility of the family meal. An eerie silence filled the room as a servant entered the room bearing a telegram. All eyes were on the message. Kira's mother opened it.

"Is it Papa?" Kira cried out.

"No." She turned to Catherine.

Catherine pushed her chair away and stood up. Kira saw the terror on her sister's face. Before Kira could reach her, Catherine's legs gave way beneath her, and she collapsed onto the floor. Without hesitation, Roman picked her up and carried her to her room. Kira took the telegram from her mother and read it.

> We sincerely regret to inform you
> that Lieutenant Georgy Karlovich
> is officially reported to have
> been killed in action.

ROMAN'S RETURN TO Crimea was a somber affair, fraught with sadness and prolonged farewells at the rail station. The following week, a garrison at Petrograd joined striking workers; combined with the bloodshed of countrymen in an unpopular and deeply disheartening war and the loss of support from the military, the Tsar was forced to abdicate.

KIRA SAT BESIDE Catherine's bedside. *She looks so peaceful.* She sighed. *If only things were* …. The door creaked open as her mother stepped into the room. "She's sleeping," Kira said.

"After all the weeping madness, the doctor gave her something to sleep."

"Will she be well enough for the journey home?"

"We will wait until her constitution has settled."

"Will you be safe with what's happening in the streets?"

"Your father is sending armed guards to escort us."

"I hate to leave her in this condition, but I need to get Anya home."

"You must go. God will keep us safe."

THE RING THAT Roman had commissioned was secured safely in Kira's luggage. She boarded the train, with a heavy heart uncertain of her sister's illness and the country's disconcertment. Everything she knew was crumbling like withered rose petals.

Kira was surprised to see so many families at the station, their anxious faces mirroring her own feelings. *I guess they also want to escape. I wonder who will be left.*

"I'm glad to be going home," Anya said. "I missed my school and friends."

"Yes, dear." Kira stared out the window of their private compartment as the train whistle blew. Her thoughts wandered to Roman as the rhythm of the wheels clickity-clacked along the tracks. She wished for his wellbeing, hoping never to receive a dreaded telegram.

The trip home was riddled with multiple stop-and-go breakdowns. When the train arrived in Siberia, Anya called out. "Who are all those soldiers? I don't recognize the uniform."

Kira stopped a porter. "Who are those soldiers?"

"Americans, Madam. They have declared war on Germany. They're here to protect the movement of supplies for the war effort."

"That's a good thing, isn't it Mother?"

"I hope so, love.

THIRTY-FIVE
1918

By SPRING, KIRA'S prayers had been answered. An armistice was signed with Germany, and Roman was home. The family met him at the train station. Roman was surprised at the flock of soldiers from different nationalities in the streets. On the sidelines, enthusiastic residents waved flags.

"Why all these soldiers?" Roman said.

"The Japanese are worried that the Bolsheviks will take control. The British and American troops have joined them."

"Maybe united we can overthrow those devils."

"It's in my nightly prayers."

VLADIVOSTOK'S SCIENTIFIC, CULTURAL, and industrial center was thriving, but underneath was a condition of lawlessness with criminal bands organized for murder and robbery. Where riots and brawls were a nightly occurrence. Roman felt a counterrevolution growing within the city. All the while, an influenza pandemic ravaged the world.

Even with all the chaos under their feet, the family maintained a balance of a daily routine of volunteerism, school, and work. But by fall, things changed dramatically. A violent revolution of soldiers, sailors, and industrial workers was underway in major cities. Word spread that the Tsar and his family had been surrendered by their guards and taken as prisoners. A tyrant named Vladimir Lenin led a new Provisional Government.

With the threat of Red aggression looming, Roman decided to relocate Kira and Anya. He felt there was no safe place left in Russia. Roman had established a friendship with a businessman in Shanghai. To him, it seemed the nearest and safest refuge.

Despite the uprising of anti-Bolsheviks, the Russian State established a White Army formed from various ranks of the Imperial Army, cabinet members, and a volunteer army from neighboring countries, including Cossacks. Rumors were rife about Kolchak arriving to take command, and Roman was eager to join him.

ONE EVENING, THE family put aside thoughts of the civil conflict to enjoying cake and coffee. With Kira by his side, Roman pulled a leather jewelry box from his inside coat pocket. "I know it's early for a birthday gift, but we want you to know how proud we are of you and how much we love you." He handed Anya the box.

Anya's hands trembled with excitement as she flipped open the lid. Cushioned in black velvet, the glimmer of a luminous ring shone bright. The center stone cast a purplish-red hue that sparkled like a hall of mirrors. Petite blue sapphires encircled the red stone with white baguette diamonds halfway down each side of the band. "It's the most exquisite thing I've ever seen." She slid the ring onto her finger and admired it.

"Karl Faberge designed it especially for you," Roman said. The center stone was a little smaller than a kopeck. "Rare diamonds are bestowed a name. This one was named after your mother, the Blood Moon of Kira. They sent the diamond to the finest gem cutters in Amsterdam, where they cut it into a unique octagon square shape called Asscher. The white, blue, and red colored gems symbolize the Imperial Russian flag."

Anya wrapped her arms around her father and then her mother. "I love you both so much. I never want this moment to be lost."

THE STENCH OF oily cigarettes mixed with body odor permeated the air. The pier at Vladivostok swarmed with potential passengers. Roman wove through the hordes of people with Kira and Anya in tow. The boat horn blast caused the crowd to rush forward. Kira lost hold of Anya's hand. She vanished in the mayhem.

"Roman, I've lost her," Kira exhaled a breathless cry. "Her hand slipped out of mine. She's gone."

"Don't panic. We'll find her. Hang on tight to the back of my belt and stay with me." Roman pushed his way against the tide of people. He searched above most heads, calling out her name. He saw a young girl alone and headed in that direction only to see that a parent had taken her away. His heart raced, amplified by the urgency. *Calm yourself. She's here somewhere.* Roman continued to call her name. In the distance, he heard the sounds of his daughter's pleas. "I see her, Kira." The three inched their way toward each other like a scene in a dramatic silent movie where the hero and heroine draw closer and closer and closer to each other.

Anya rushed to her father, wrapped her arms around his waist, and buried her face in his chest. "I was so scared, Papa." Her voice muffled in his shirt.

Roman said. "This is a lesson for the both of you. It's vital to stay together, especially since you will be alone in a foreign land." He hugged them both. "You must hurry and board."

"I can't bear to leave you." Kira embraced her husband.

"It's like watching a house you built burn, but I must do what I can to put it out, even though it might be futile." He kissed the top of her head.

"Roman, who will we be without a country?" her voice trembled.

Anya started to cry. Roman attempted to reassure her, "It will only be for a little while." His words felt hollow, knowing he might not see them for months, years—or worse. "I will be meeting with Kolchak in Siberia to fight the Socialist revolutionaries. He will be our savior rescuing our country."

Roman hugged his wife and kissed her on both cheeks. "I have sent a telegram to Monsieur Chiu letting him know when you will arrive in Shanghai. He will meet you at the dock. You have his information I wrote down?"

"Yes, it's in my bag."

"He will help you find a place to live. The household items should arrive within a week of your arrival. I was able to secure second-class accommodations at the last minute." Roman was relieved not to have put them in steerage, which was often congested with less than humane conditions. "I have also provided you with access to a bank in Shanghai."

Kira bit her lip to suppress tears as she took Anya by the hand. She was torn between escaping the madness and the sadness of leaving behind everything she knew. Lugging elaborately designed tapestry bags stuffed with clothing and toiletries, they trudged up the wooden plank and boarded the steamship.

The stunning ship was of an older style. Three enormous puffed-up white sails filled the sky. Grey smoke billowed from two tall black stacks. People scurried along the polished deck to find an open spot along the railing. Men on the dock removed the boarding plank. A sharp horn blasted, causing Anya to jump.

"It's all right, dear. It's to let the people know that the ship is about to leave."

They stood shoulder to shoulder with other passengers and waved at Roman. He blew them a kiss as the ship slowly departed from the dock.

"Oh, Mother, will we ever see Papa again?"

"Yes, dear." Kira bit her bottom lip with the hope her words were a prophecy.

AFTER SEVERAL DAYS aboard the ship, Kira wrote in her diary about the events they encountered so Roman could experience their journey when he rejoined them.

> We have a double bed and basin in the room but share a washroom with several others. I am thankful for the accommodations, as the decks below echo cries from children and alarming moans. The sea is not very forgiving for some. Even our poor Anya has been struck by *mal de mer.* I gave her some ginger and soda to help ease her stomach.
>
> I have met a couple who fled from St. Petersburg. They say things are terrible and not any better in Moscow. People are without food and shelter. And there is no fuel to cook or heat the home—if you are lucky to still have a home. It seems some people feel they have a right to anyone's property. I am glad that Auntie is not alive to see it. My heart aches with worry for my family. I hope they were able

to make their way to France as planned.

The ship stopped in Busan for a day. We were not allowed to disembark, but along the rails, we saw the hills with homes stacked close together. The men wear strange black hats. It has a tall cylindrical shape and a wide brim with ribbons that tie around the chin.

We should be arriving in Shanghai within the week. It's been an interesting adventure. The Chinese crewmembers, who seem to be the backbone of this ship, are commanded by European officers. They apparently don't speak the same language. I have observed the officers using hand signals to communicate orders.

I'm off to dinner with our new acquaintances. I long to hold Roman in my arms.

Kira placed her journal on the nightstand.

KIRA CHANGED INTO a muted olive two-piece lace evening gown with half-length sleeves and slid on long evening gloves. Anya, feeling better, wore a white dress with a full skirt cut several inches above the ankle.

Kira and Anya entered the dining room. When not set up for dining, the room was used for passengers to play cards or board games. They were met by the steward, who guided them across the floral-designed purple and green carpet to a square linen-draped table for four. Already seated were the couple from St. Petersburg. The grey-bearded man had a stately air about him. His wife was a pleasant woman with a round face and matronly shape. Their attire and manner were that of having some wealth.

Kira sat on a purple plush chair. "Good evening," An older couple had already been seated at the table. The steward laid a white linen napkin on her lap and handed her a menu. She scanned the menu. "I think the fish is a solid choice. What do you think, Anya?"

Anya shrugged.

"Sit up, dear. How about a simple broth?"

"And bread would be fine," Anya said.

"What are your plans once you arrive in Shanghai?" Kira directed her question to the couple.

The man refused to answer. Kira didn't mind his arrogance. She was happy to have company.

"To be honest, we don't have any firm plans," the woman responded. "We had to leave everything behind and escaped with only the things we could carry. I sewed all my jewels in garments, but most were confiscated … stolen … as we traveled to get here. But at least we have our lives, unlike many of our friends who were shot."

"I remember when my husband moved us to Vladivostok. I was so distraught at leaving my family. I look at it now and marvel at his perceptiveness. We've been fortunate to retain most of our possessions."

The husband held up his glass for the server. "Replenish." He spoke to him as if he were his serf, pretending to live the life he was forced to leave.

If he does not bend with the new times, his life will forever be miserable.

THIRTY-SIX

ROMAN STOOD ANCHORED to the pier. Melancholy filled his soul as he watched his wife and daughter sail out of sight. The uncertain future, with the possibility of Kolchak's return to challenge the Bolsheviks, kept him in Vladivostok. Kira's words twisted about in his mind, 'Without a country, who are we?'

The war had profoundly transformed the city and its outlying areas, and with it, foreign concerns about their interests grew. British, American, French, and Canadian troops had been dispatched. Buildings that once held theater productions and schools of learning were used as barracks, their once vibrant facades now marred by signs of war. Roman struggled to get around with the mass of foreign soldiers parading along the streets. A sign that the Russians had lost control of the Vladivostok. It now lay in the hands of the Japanese, a significant shift in the power dynamics of the war. He and the others simply waited for Kolchak.

Nights were incredibly lonely. Roman drank most of his evening meals lounging in the only remaining piece of furniture, a well-worn, overstuffed chair. The rest of the household items had been sent to Shanghai. He looked out the large paned window of their apartment toward the port and further across the bay. His thoughts drifted to Kira and Anya. He hoped their crossing had been without incident. He perused the local paper, reading about infighting among the Bolsheviks. Lenin had been seriously wounded by an assassination attempt. The assassin, a woman, had called him a traitor before she fired a pistol. According to the report, she got off three rounds. Roman believed that Lenin was vulnerable, which, in his opinion, made their victory more probable.

ROMAN WRESTLED THROUGH a stack of requisition papers on his office desk. He had to account for the military equipment they would need to take to Siberia. He heard the clacking of heels racing down the hall.

An out-of-breath clerk entered the room and spoke. "Someone … someone is here to see you, Sir."

Roman looked up. He jerked his head back with widened eyes as Uri stood in the doorway. He had not heard from Uri for several years, believing he had been killed. Roman dashed around the desk, grabbed his friend by the arm, and drew him in with a firm embrace.

"I don't believe it. How? Why?" Roman said.

"I watched as my friends, my comrades, my

brothers, turn over the Tsar and his family to those animals." Uri's voice quaked with emotion as his eyes welled up. "I had to get away."

"I am sorry." Roman patted his shoulder. "Is your family with you?"

Uri lowered his head and spoke softly. "My wife died a few months ago from influenza. Unfortunately, my son also contracted it." His voice cracked.

"I'm truly sorry." Roman reached into his desk drawer and pulled out a bottle of vodka and two glasses. He poured a splash into each and handed one to Uri. They downed their shots.

"How about we get out of here and find a place for a proper drink." Roman took Uri by the arm and led him out of the room.

THE TWO SAT at a dark corner table in a local smoked-filled tavern away from prying ears. Roman sipped Ararat brandy. "You know that Kolchak will arrive here in the next several days."

Uri nodded. "Yes. That's why I decided to make the trek. To hook up with him and go after those red devils. And, in hope that you'd still be here." Uri paused. "What about Kira?"

"I sent her and Anya to China ... along with hundreds of fleeing Russians."

"Good. I'm glad they're safe."

"How's Ivan?"

Uri looked away. "I am so sorry, Roman. The

horse doctor said it was colic. Most likely a toxin in the hay. Several other horses were also affected."

Roman rubbed Uri's shoulder. He felt his throat close up and forced the tears back. "Any word from Fëdor or Boris?"

"Fëdor was involved in quelling a violent protest. It was reported that he fell off his horse, more like pulled off, and then beaten to death by the mob." Uri shook his head. "And you know Boris. He got caught up in some kind of a squabble about him having to pledge allegiance to the new rule. Of course, being an aristocrat, he refused … they shot him on the spot. Middle of the day. Middle of the road. Middle of a crowd. Beginning of a nightmare." Uri downed his drink and refilled his glass. "I think they would have shot him regardless. It's the French revolution all over again."

The two remained silent for a moment before Roman raised his glass. "Here's to the musketeers and ending the nightmare."

THE DAY HAD finally arrived, and everyone was in a flurry as Kolchak's ship docked. Several ranking officers, along with Roman and Uri, went to the pier to meet him. Roman recognized Kolchak's recognizable long black wool coat with a leather belt cinched at the waist and his high boots. The grimace on his face as he approached told them all they needed to know—rough times were on the horizon.

The dignitaries crowded around Kolchak. He spotted Roman and grabbed his arms. "I'm glad that you'll be with us, my friend."

Roman said, "It is my honor, Sir."

Kolchak took Roman to the side," They murdered the Tsar and his family."

The news hit Roman like a sharp pain piercing his chest as if something had impaled it.

"It was on Lenin's order. He's also moved the capital to Moscow."

Roman grasped Kolchak's upper arm. "Together, we will annihilate those vermin."

Kolchak nodded and then faced the crowd. "It is good to be among you. I have longed to see my country again and the chance to rid the pestilence that has consumed our homeland."

Noisy cheers arose.

They left the pier and headed to a quaint eatery, where arrangements were made for a farewell feast. Over the next few days, they would prepare to head out by rail to Omsk.

THIRTY-SEVEN

Shanghai

BUNDLED IN FUR-collared woolen coats and fur hats, Kira and Anya stood against the deck railing. The radiant sun warmed their faces as the ship entered the Huangpu River. The river snaked along until it reached its final bend, revealing a modern city. They stood in awe at the striking sight of tall Western-style buildings, fashionable automobiles, and a mixture of Europeans and Chinese dressed in Western attire. This ship's horn emitted a loud, deep reverberating blast.

"Oh, Mother. I was so worried it would be awful, but it isn't. Shanghai is beautiful."

"Yes, dear. It reminds me of St Petersburg or Moscow … even Paris. Aren't we lucky? But we must be discreet regarding our financial situation. Many families have traveled here with nothing."

They lingered a few more minutes, absorbing their

surroundings, before returning to their cabin to make final preparations for disembarkation.

KIRA HAD BARELY set one foot on land when a slender Chinese man removed his hat and bowed before her. "Madame Pavlovitch?"

"Monsieur Chiu?" She remembered that Roman had given her his information.

He bowed again and spoke to them in French with a heavy Chinese accent. "It is nice to meet you. Your husband is a great friend." He bowed. "I will help you to the Astor House." He rushed them along to a waiting sedan.

"But … our luggage?"

"No worries. It will follow later."

The driver stopped in front of a multi-story brick building in the neo-classic style. "Welcome to the Astor House Hotel," Chiu said.

"What are we doing here?" Kira said.

"Your house is not ready. Your furniture is expected to arrive next week. In the meantime, you may reside at this fashionable hotel."

Heavy mahogany chairs and side tables in the arched lobby gave the impression of entering a clandestine spy ring. Kira thought the men lounging looked as sinister as the décor.

Chiu returned from the registration desk. "Let us have tea while they prepare your room."

Kira dismissed the server and poured everyone's

tea. Chiu refused milk and sugar. A tier of sandwiches, cakes, and frosted petit fours had been ordered. Anya helped herself to several cakes.

Chui took a sip. "I have a daughter about your age, Miss Anya. I think she would very much like to meet you."

Anya could hardly contain herself and barely finished her bite of cake. "That would be marvelous." She held her hand to her mouth and coughed. "When can we meet?"

"Manners, dear. We need to get settled before we venture off."

Anya fell back in her seat. "Yes, Mother."

"I will leave you to finish your tea and call on you tomorrow," Chui said.

After tea, Kira and Anya followed the hotel porter down a long Victorian hallway with an odd Tudor-style flair. Their room had high ceilings with a double bed, chaise, and chair. Their luggage sat on an area rug that lay over hardwood floors. Floor-to-ceiling velvet drapes adorned the windows. A fragrant waft filled the room from a vase of freshly cut flowers.

"Dinner service starts at eight, Madame," the porter said.

Kira handed him a few *yuan* before he left the room.

KIRA AND ANYA entered the great dining room, where white linen cloths draped rows of tables. Four

Bentwood chairs with caned seats were arranged around each table, along with elaborate china and crystal glassware.

The maître d' escorted them to a corner table apart from other couples. Kira believed it was because they were not accompanied by a man. A reluctant waiter approached their table. Kira smiled at him and his shoulders relaxed.

A short, rotund European man dressed in a white suit passed them. Kira observed his pyramid mustache. It reminded her of Colonel Vershinin. She shuddered at the thought. The waiter addressed him with a slight head bow. His nervousness was apparent to Kira. When the man was out of earshot, the waiter leaned in and whispered, "That was the owner. He is a very important businessman."

After dinner, they retired to their room. Kira sat and wrote in her journal before retiring to bed.

> We arrived in the enchanting city of Shanghai today. Monsieur Chui met us at the dock and has kindly offered to take us on a tour tomorrow so we may become familiar with the area. We are currently staying at a hotel until our home is ready. I was fascinated to hear multiple languages being spoken at the same time. Apparently, wealthy businessmen from all parts of the world stay here.
>
> We met the hotel owner during dinner this evening. He is a funny little man who pulls at his mustache. Monsieur Chiu works for the Chinese Press, which also owns the hotel. I

believe it's the reason we are staying here. Our room is quite adequate, but I am eager to be in a home surrounded by my things.

Anya is reading *Anna Karenina* for the fourth time. I fear she misses her opportunity as a debutant. These past few weeks, she has matured into a lovely young lady. I am so proud of the young woman she is becoming. The Chui's have a daughter who is near her age. I hope they will become companions. Anya needs to be with young ladies of a like age.

We heard on the wireless that the war is over. The news filled us with a mix of relief and joy. Everyone on the ship cheered. To commemorate, champagne was served at dinner.

I pray Roman will send us a note that he has found victory, and we may soon return to Russia.

THE FOLLOWING DAY, Chiu had a sedan waiting. A young Chinese girl stood next to the vehicle.

"Miss Anya, may I present my eldest daughter, Bia Chiu."

Bia appeared different from the Chinese girls Anya had met in the north. She was smaller, darker-skinned, with a flatter nose and eyelids that angled downward. "I am so pleased to meet you," Anya said.

Bia bowed her head. Anya's attention was drawn to the cheongsam Bia wore. It was navy blue satin with petite white flowers and knotted buttons along the mandarin collar. "I so admire your dress. Maybe one day you could help me pick one out."

"My mother made this for me." Bia paused. "Maybe she could make one for you."

"Oh, that would be wonderful."

Kira settled in the front seat. Anya and Bia were in the back, where the two continued their incessant chatter as Chiu drove off.

"I want to show you the beautiful architecture that Shanghai has to offer and for you to become acquainted with the neighborhoods."

They drove along narrow, twisting lanes lined with jewelry stores, clothing shops, and tea houses. Kira observed the vast construction of tall buildings and residences.

"Madame Kira, this may be of interest." They stopped in front of a church. "This is Saint Ignatius Cathedral, built by French Jesuits a few years ago. Many Europeans attend its services."

"Yes, thank you. I would be most interested in attending."

They drove on. "And here," he pointed to the right. "We have elegant classic architecture from the Ming and Qing dynasties."

Kira admired the pink façade and black roofs with graceful, upswept eaves. She noted how harmoniously they intermingled with several European-style buildings.

They continued to traverse the city while Chiu proudly explained the nuance of each site. "We shall stop at Yuyuan Garden for tea. It is a tranquil place with elaborate pavilions, glittering pools, and impressive rockeries. It was designed by a son for his parents—centuries ago.

They walked across a zig-zag bridge that led to a round pavilion stationed on stilts.

"I'm feeling dizzy," Anya said as she swayed.

Chiu said, "The layout is intended to ward off evil spirits as they can only travel in a straight line." He smiled.

They sat at a table next to small-paned windows. A mixture of various spicy aromas lingered in the air. The interior woodwork was painted a deep red, and the ceiling glowed yellow from artificial light cast upward. After tea, Chiu took them back to their hotel.

On the way to their room, Kira said to Anya. "How did you like Bia?"

"Oh, I liked her. She is very intelligent and wants to travel the world. One day we plan to see Paris."

Kira smiled and admired Anya's aspiration.

THIRTY-EIGHT
Omsk

ROMAN AND URI awoke on a bitterly cold, ashen-gray morning. The kind of day where the dampness seeps into your bones. "This city has a graveyard chill to it," Roman said.

Stomachs rumbled as the two ventured in search of a meal. Omsk was under Kolchak's control. Upon his arrival, he had executed a military *coup d'état*. Those who opposed were either shot or beaten and imprisoned.

Roman's boots sloshed along the muddy walkway. "I'm concerned." He sighed. "The capture of the city was brutal. I fear we won't win the support of the countrymen if we continue in this manner. We need every able body to defeat the Reds."

"Those who are not partisan are the enemy … insects, vermin, and lice to be squashed. The Red

Terror massacres our brothers in arms. Think of Fëdor and Boris. Blood must be shed."

Roman nodded. "Let's hope it's a one-time occurrence and local conflict will be handled more diplomatically in the future." It was his wish, but the uncertainty of future events cast a shadow of doubt.

"I heard some of the troops are moving west to Perm," Uri said.

Roman nodded. "Kolchak wants to capture as much territory as possible before the frigidity of winter sets in." Roman vigorously rubbed his hands together and blew his breath on them. "Let's find a tavern with a blazing fire."

RELAXING BESIDE A roaring fireplace, the two sipped their *Sbiten* with a splash of vodka added. Roman wrapped his hands around the glass to warm his fingers. The fire cast a glow on his troubled face. He continued with his thoughts from earlier. "The problem with this army is too many divisions of leadership and independent factions. Our leaders are not helping. They've become more autocratic, causing friction among the factions. The Czechs are discontented with their need for independence from Bohemia. With the overtaking of Omsk and hopefully Perm, things might improve. We have socialists who just don't like the Bolsheviks. And the peasantry simply want food on the table. There is no shared ideology. Everyone is looking out for themselves and what they can get out of this war."

Uri furrowed his brow. "You seem disillusioned."

"I'm concerned whether we can reach Moscow with this army. If we generate goodwill we would win their loyalty. I wish Kolchak would take heed."

"What do you intend to do?"

"What can I do but obey my commander?"

They continued to sip their drinks and stared into the hypnotic flames.

ROMAN WAS AWAKENED by a thunderous stampede. He jumped from his cot and threw open the front tent flap. Men's faces covered in grime and dressed in what were once shirts and pants, now filthy rags, scurried in all directions.

Uri sat up. "What is it?"

"Prisoners escaping."

They threw on pants and grabbed their rifles. By the time they got outside, the prisoners were no longer in sight. Screams from civilians echoed in their ears. They ran down the street. Rapid gunfire stopped them. Guns readied. They ran toward the commotion and saw troops open fire on the crowd.

"There must be more than 200 in the crowd," Uri said.

"And not all of them are prisoners."

A haze of smoke and a sulfuric odor lingered in the air after the gunfire stopped. Roman approached an officer. "What happened?"

"A group of anti-Bolsheviks liberated the prisoners. We were ordered to stop them. Now we will hunt down the instigators."

Roman's stomach twisted. He steadied his breathing as he stared at the carnage of blood and mangled bodies of women and children that besieged the streets. He noticed a few soldiers were visibly disturbed by the sight while others rummaged through clothing, looking for valuables.

Uri put his hand on Roman's back. "There is nothing we can do here. Let's head back."

"We are never going to win over the people." Roman hung his head. "This war was lost before it even began."

NEWS FROM THE commanders in Perm reported that they had secured the area. Kolchak arrived in the industrial city. Roman and Uri stood with a welcome group as the bitter cold winter nipped at their skin. A smile crossed Kolchak's face when the officers showed him the captured flotilla frozen in the Kama River. Roman could tell the Admiral was sizing up the captured assets of tug boats that had been transformed into gunboats and steamers reinforced with armor plates and equipped with cannons.

Uri nudged Roman. "It seems your concerns over the army's abilities were proven unfounded."

"Let's hope."

A lean man of medium height approached Roman.

He scrutinized the stranger's light blue eyes when the man extended his hand.

"Paval Nikolaevich. I am a local reporter for the newspaper, covering Kolchak's arrival in Perm."

Roman shook Paval's warm hand. "I see the town has honored Kolchak with a parade."

"And deservedly so," Paval said. "Were you here when the army took control of Perm?"

"No."

"It was glorious. The Red Army surrendered within days. Seems they'd been sent into battle without adequate training or winter clothing. Their troops were suffering from food shortages, a consequence of disorganization and alienation of the peasantry by the Red Terror. This is all very promising for Kolchak. It suggests that the Red Army might be on the brink of disintegration."

Roman remained silent, unwilling to dampen Paval's enthusiasm.

Uri smiled. "I could use a drink. Let's find a tavern."

"PAVAL, WHAT ARE you reporting about?" Uri gulped down a shot of vodka.

"The events. I not only want the people but also my children to know the truth about what happened to our country."

Roman sat back in his chair. "You know, if we fail, the Reds will hunt you down and shoot you."

"We must all be prepared to sacrifice. Isn't it your duty to be victorious?"

Uri broke out with a rowdy laugh.

Roman gulped a shot. "I like you, Paval. I do. But you need to be prepared."

"The Great War is over worldwide. Maybe now we will finally receive the much needed aid from western nations," Paval said.

"Many are war-weary and may not have the will," Roman said.

"Enough of this gloom." Uri raised his glass. "A toast. To victory."

THIRTY-NINE

Shanghai

DRIVING THROUGH SYCAMORE-LINED avenues and narrow streets, Kira admired the homes, ranging from villas to country-style. Many of their wood sidings were painted a vibrant red with lush ivy crawling up the exteriors. She felt her spirits lift at the familiarity of the surroundings.

"This is known as the French Concession. The trees were imported from France," Chiu pointed out. "There are many food and apparel shops for your pleasure. You will be quite safe to walk alone in this area."

He stopped the car in front of a white stucco building. "I have procured a lovely apartment for you on the third floor."

Kira entered the building's foyer. "No lift?" She calculated the number of stairs. "I guess this will improve our constitutions."

Kira caught her breath before entering the residence. It opened to spacious living quarters with a kitchen at one end and bedrooms down an opposite hall. Their furniture had been set up. Several boxes marked with kitchenware, linens, and knickknacks were stacked across the floor, which drove home the sense of relocation.

Anya stood in front of the window, looking at the row of buildings across the street, and sighed. "I miss the view of the sea."

Removing her coat and gloves, Kira placed them on the davenport. "We all have to adjust, dear."

"Yes, Mother." She flopped down in a chair. "When will Father be with us?"

Kira hesitated. "I suspect he will call us back home in a few months."

Anya pursed her lips and furrowed her brow. "Given all the refugees pouring into Shanghai, I believe it's more likely he would be joining us."

MONTHS PASSED, AND still no word from Roman. Anya's melancholy mood concerned Kira.

"What's the matter, Anya?" Kira stared at her daughter, who sat at the kitchen table with her head hung. Her face rested in her hands. "Is it your father?"

"I witnessed a terrible thing today." Anya's voice had taken on a shrill tone.

Weakened knees forced Kira to sit. "What?"

"I was shopping at the food store. A woman, a

refugee around your age, snatched a loaf of bread and stuffed it in her coat. Her cold-lifeless eyes looked into mine. It was like looking at the walking dead. And without expression, as if nothing had happened, she walked away. I felt a shiver go up my spine."

"Did you report her?"

Anya shook her bowed head. "That's not the horror. She was a respectable-looking woman. I thought, why is she stealing? So I followed her."

"I'm not sure I approve of that action." Kira reached over and caressed Anya's hand.

"I wasn't thinking about anything except what would possess a person to do such a thing. She went down an alley and stopped midway. Huddled along the side were four young children. She removed the bread from beneath her coat and split it amongst them without taking a share for herself."

Anya squeezed her mother's hand. "They were starving." A tear fell onto the table. 'I gave her what money I had. She was forever grateful. Oh, Mother. We need to help them." Anya raised her head and looked at her mother. She wiped the tears from her cheeks. Her eyes widened. "Why are you dressed in a gown?"

"I met a couple who were friends of your Aunt Masha. They've invited me to a gala with several fellow Russians.

"Mother, have you been listening to what I saw?"

"Yes, dear. But we need to socialize to maintain

some kind of a normal life while we are here." Kira rose from her seat and straightened her dress.

Anya's face turned Russian red. "We need to do something to help the starving."

"It's quite dark outside. There isn't anything we can do at this time."

Anya jumped out of her seat. A loud bang reverberated when the chair crashed to the floor. "There by the grace … Mother."

"Anya, please pick up the chair and go to your room. We will talk tomorrow once you've calmed down." Without obeying her mother's command, Anya stomped off.

She misses her father. Kira put on her coat and gloves, tucked her evening bag under her arm, and left.

THE EVENING WAS more than Kira had expected. She found herself surrounded by elegance, with white linen table settings that filled the room and crystal chandeliers casting an amber hue on those below. A solo cellist played Bach while people dined.

Kira sipped champagne and turned to the couple in their late fifties beside her. "It's as if Russia has come to us." She said. "And in some strange way, it has."

"Most are dignitaries from other countries. Russians dressed in their finery escaped several years earlier. They were able to retain most of their wealth." The woman paused. "You see the couple at the far end table?"

Kira nodded.

"They arrived several months ago. The husband has a fake tooth where he wedged in a highly prized alexandrite. The sale fetched enough to buy a cottage and money to live on for some time."

Kira thought back to her conversation with Anya. "My daughter saw a woman and her children starving in the streets. She wants to help them but I'm not sure what can be done."

"There is a humanity of Russian immigrants who get together at Saint Ignatius and provide meals for those in need. If your daughter would like to contribute, I believe all she needs to do is show up with a cooked meal."

"Thank you. I will mention it to her."

A shadow passed Kira's line of sight. She looked up to see an impeccably dressed man hovering over their table. He presented himself to the couple.

"Mrs. Pavlovitch, may I introduce Baron Sidorov."

He was not tall, with gray around the temples and a bit of mischief in his eyes. The Baron took her hand and kissed it. "*Enchanté.*"

His familiarity made her pull away. A polite smile crossed her lips.

He pulled a chair from another table and sat beside her. He conversed with the couple for a few minutes then turned to Kira. "You look upset, Madame."

Kira felt a wave of uneasiness at his imprudence in addressing her in such a manner. *Well, it's not a secret that I'm desperate for help. Anyone's help.* "I've been trying to reach word about my parents through the French Embassy. I want to see if they arrived in Paris. I go weekly to see if there is any word—but nothing."

"Maybe I can help. I am acquainted with the French consul." He rose. "I will be in touch in a few days." He bowed and walked away.

The woman spoke. "He says he is a Baron, but who knows these days."

"I don't recognize him, but then I've been away from St. Petersburgh's court for several years. However, it begs the question of why he is here and not back home fighting to save our country."

FORTY

Omsk 1919

ROMAN SQUATTED ON his heels to avoid sitting on the muddy ground. His mind filled with worry for Kira and Anya. He hoped they were well-situated in Shanghai. Uri's sudden, loud, long cough interrupted his thoughts.

"Are you all right? That cough has been persistent for over a week."

Uri silenced the whooping. "Something in the air."

"What do you think of Kolchak's appointment as Supreme Ruler of Russia?"

Uri rubbed his facial stubble. "We've had tremendous progress in controlling Siberia," he coughed and cleared his throat, "although the sacrifice made in capturing Perm has been high. Our fortune has been that the Reds were outflanked and forced to retreat. But with aid from Britain and America, I think it was a wise move to elect Kolchak." A wide grin grew across his face. "You know, we just might win this war."

"I'm concerned about the Czechs and Cossacks. They are complaining about Kolchak's autocratic rule. Dissension within the splintered groups might give the Reds the upper hand. We need to keep a watchful eye."

"Agreed."

A sickly sweet odor with a hint of rotting fish lingered in the air—the kind of smell one never forgets. Roman stood up as a procession of reindeer sleds slushed past. Piled aboard were the critically injured and dead. Those still alive had gangrenous wounds— worms crawled about their injuries.

"Where the hell are they taking them?" Uri said.

Roman could barely swallow. "There's a Red Cross camp a few miles away."

They looked at each other in silence. A sickness twisted in Roman's stomach. The acrid sting of war was taking its toll. He longed to run from the horror.

As spring advanced, so did the ideology of the Whites. They gained significant ground to the south while Kolchak led the army west toward Moscow. The initial progress sparked hope. However, by the end of spring, the fighting had regressed. In response to the army's brutality, the peasantry began to oppose. The Reds focused on fragmented groups, as Roman had feared. They cut off the center forces, forcing Kolchak to retreat east of the Urals.

Before leaving Perm, Uri and Roman shared a

fond farewell drink with Paval.

"Since I have been reporting against the Bolsheviks, they have placed me on a 'shoot on-sight' list. I plan to take my family and escape to Germany and then on to the Americas."

"We wish you luck," Roman said as the three clinked their glasses.

AS SUPPLY LINES began to falter, morale steadily declined. A swell of desertions had become a pandemic. Orders had come down to shoot deserters, but Roman could not face shooting someone in the back. He figured it was better to be without them than have them remain disgruntled in the ranks. The truth was, he coveted their freedom and felt the urge to follow, a pull that grew stronger as the war efforts began to bog down.

Uri's constant coughing and headaches alarmed Roman. When Uri could no longer keep any sustenance down, Roman took him to the infirmary.

"He has a high fever and a rash spreading across his back and chest. I'm afraid it's typhus," the doctor said. "The war has delivered this plague. You see the ward is filled. There's a plethora of ticks and fleas in every blanket in every household."

Roman observed that the infirmary beds were filled with men in the same condition, and the bitter smells of antiseptic undertones permeated the air.

"What can be done, doctor?"

"Nothing at this point. It's up to him. We can only pray and wait for the infection to run its course."

THE WARMTH OF the summer months brought new optimism to Roman … that and word of American officials meeting with Kolchak. Roman hoped reinforcements would be coming as provisions were at their weakest point. Filthy garments that were once uniforms hung off skeleton soldiers—every day, more and more deserted. And the flood of refugees devoured what little food and supplies remained.

Uri's condition had worsened. Roman spent his free time at his friend's bedside. He recited the day's news even though Uri's delirium drifted in and out of consciousness.

"I fear the war will end soon and not to our advantage. Foreign aid is too slow in coming. The Americans have withdrawn from the Red Cross. They didn't want their nurses stranded in Siberia."

Uri stirred. Roman tucked the blanket under his chin.

"Oh, Uri, what a mess we're in. They are burning villages where the peasantry disobeys. The disobedient are locked up and not fed. Rather than let them go, they remain prisoners, starving by the hundreds. Villages are complaining of the bullet-ridden bodies rotting in the fields. The stench unfathomable, and they say they can't plant. I told one villager he should obtain a gas mask as they would need the grain to feed themselves. This type of brutality is why I left for the Far East." He hung his head. "But I forget that we are fighting to restore the monarchy ... or are we? I wonder how we will be measured for our efforts here. The monarchy has brought Russia to ruin. But I refuse to believe the alternative is better."

A soldier, rushed into the ward and summoned him to report to Kolchak for a meeting.

Roman entered the crowded room, the air heavy with tension. Several men, many not Russians, sat around a long table. Those who spoke English, he assumed, were the Americans. A stocky silver-haired gentleman with a soft-spoken manner expressed concern about several high-ranking officers' lack of control in Siberia. "Why do they refuse to use the Japanese army, who outnumber them, for assistance?" the man said. Kolchak immediately dismissed the suggestion. Before Roman could sit, a nurse entered the room and motioned for Roman. Roman glanced over at Kolchak, who nodded his approval.

The doctor met Roman at the entrance to the ward. "I'm afraid it's his time. You need to say your goodbyes now."

Roman looked down at Uri. A robust body that once sat tall in a saddle was now weatherworn, like a man years beyond his age. He remembered when they were young cadets recruited into the Imperial Guard. Their hearts brimmed with hope for a future they would shape. How proud they were to guard the Tsar and Tsarina. How Boris, Fëdor, Uri, and he, the musketeers, reveled in their friendship. Then, as quickly as it came, it was gone—withered leaves from a deciduous tree.

"My dear, dear friend. Our time together has come to an end. I wish you well on your journey. I too have a journey. I plan to reunite with Kira and Anya. This mess of a war that has affected all our lives is all but over as seen by the mass defections." Roman's heart ached as he sat in silence, watching Uri's life slip away with each breath.

THE AMERICANS LEFT Siberia in September. Roman wondered if they would ever see any results from their promises. Months dragged on, and still nothing was forthcoming from the Americans or British. By late fall, Kolchak loaded several train cars with what treasures they had left and headed east. Roman decided that no matter Kolchak's plan, he would continue to Vladivostok and catch a freighter for Shanghai. Mother Russia was lost. His loyalty now lay with his family.

FORTY-ONE

Shanghai

A TINNY SOUND rang from the bell box attached to the black candlestick telephone. Kira picked up the cylindrical neck of the base in one hand, lifted the receiver from the switch hook with the other, and placed it to her ear. She spoke into the mouthpiece. "Hello."

"Madame Pavlovitch." The voice on the other end crackled.

Her face flushed at the sound of a strange man's voice. "Yes."

"Baron Sidorov, here."

"Oh, yes."

"I have wonderful news about your family. Can we meet today for lunch at the Astor House?"

Kira hesitated. Her mind reeled. Unsure if she should agree.

"Hello, are you there?"

Her determination to learn the truth about her parent's fate outweighed her caution. "Yes. I'll see you there." She placed the receiver back on the hook and set the telephone down.

"Who was that?" Anya said.

"Someone who has information about my parents in Paris."

"Who?"

"A man I met at dinner the other night." Kira rushed to her room to change clothes.

"Maybe I should come along."

"Don't be silly. It's only lunch. Besides, isn't Bia coming over to help you prepare a meal for the church?"

Anya followed her mother and rested on the bed. "Why didn't he simply tell you what he knew over the telephone?"

Kira stopped for a moment. "I don't know. In all the excitement, I didn't think to ask." She piled her hair on top of her head and pinned it. She had not mustered the courage to bob her hair like Anya. Kira grabbed her coat and gloves, kissed Anya on the cheek, and raced out the door.

THE TAXICAB BARELY came to a stop as Kira swung open the door, not waiting for the hotel doorman's assistance, and rushed up the steps. She took a moment to catch her breath and straighten her dress before entering the dining room. The Baron sat at a corner table. He rose from his seat as she approached. His eyes scrutinized her.

"*Enchanté.*" He kissed her gloved hand and pulled a chair out for her. Kira noticed a bottle of Louis Roederer Cristal that rested in an ice bucket.

"What news have you, Baron?" Kira removed her gloves and placed them on her lap.

"First, we must drink." He filled the glasses to the brim. "A toast. *Tchin-tchin.*" Their glasses clinked together.

Kira took a sip. But before she could utter a word—

"I have taken the liberty to order our meal. Discussions are better digested on a full stomach—no?" He smiled a toothy grin.

He has a nice smile with heart-shaped lips, she thought. *He appears much younger than I remembered. I'm somewhat flattered by his attention, but I'm a married woman and shouldn't have such thoughts.* She shifted in her seat. *When are we going to get to the news about my family?*

Lunch started with oysters on the half-shell. Kira wanted to rush through the meal, but modern decorum would not permit her to gobble her food.

The conversation was a testament to his free spirit. Kira listened attentively as he expounded on his quest to see as many ancient archaeological sites as possible. He had scaled atop the great pyramid at Giza, beheld the buried remains at Pompeii, roamed around Por-

Bazhy, a mysterious island fortress, and journeyed on a camel through the Jordanian desert to admire the hand-carved sandstone cliffs of Petra. She wondered why he had never married, never settled, a nomad at best … a man without a country—homeless. She felt a sense of pity for him.

He slurped down the last oyster before he spoke. "I was in Shanghai when news about the Tsars and his family's murder. I decided it was better to stay in Shanghai until the world quietened."

A Niçoise salad with a white fish was served. The Baron droned on about his exploits, continually filling their glasses. Kira's mind wandered. She looked around at all the wealth and prestige in one room. She thought about Anya's concern for the refugees.

Dessert arrived. The server poured the batter into a heated chafing dish, tipping the pan from side to side to spread the batter thinly. He folded the crepe into a triangle, placed it on a side dish, and prepared several more. He returned all the crepes to the pan, poured in brandy, and lit it. It ignited a flame that shot up a good foot. When the fire died down, he served the crepe suzette. Before dessert ended, Kira could feel the wine taking its effect.

Kira could no longer hold her tongue as soon as the plates were removed. "I appreciate the lunch, Baron, but I really need to hear what you discovered about my family."

"Yes, dear." He patted her hand.

His tone sounded condescending. Kira removed her hand from the table and placed it on her lap. She lent him a smile that could coax a man into saying or doing anything.

He yielded to her wish. "My contact in Paris said there was a man, wife, and two daughters under the name Aleksandrovich who registered with the embassy. But he didn't know if they remained in France or migrated to England or the Americas."

Kira's brow furrowed. "You said two daughters?"

"Yes."

"But … I have three sisters. Are you sure?"

"I'm sorry. That's what was relayed to me."

The news struck her like a thunderbolt, jolting her into sobriety. Her voice shaking, she asked. "Is there any way I might speak with this person?"

"I can arrange for you to speak to someone at the French consulate, but there's no guarantee the person knows more than what I've told you.

"I understand. I need assurance that this is my family, which sister is missing, and why." She put her gloves on to leave.

"I also left information on where to contact you directly if they hear from your family."

Kira placed her gloved hand on his and squeezed it. "Thank you."

KIRA WALKED INTO the apartment after lunch. She could smell the lingering aroma of beef stew and wondered if Anya had delivered it to the church. Her mind quickly shifted to thoughts about her parents.

Anya raced into the room with enough energy to light a bulb. She twirled around. "Look at what Bia's mother made for me. It's a real Cheongsam."

Kira admired the vibrant red silk brocade gown and the beautifully hand-embroidered stitching with knotted buttons that crossed the bodice. A tear came to Kira's eye at the sight of the tailored form that revealed the figure of a young woman.

Anya noticed the sorrowful expression on her mother's face. "What's the matter? Don't you like it?"

"It's lovely, dear." Kira wrung her hands.

"Did something happen during lunch?"

Kira did not respond.

"Mother. Why did you meet that man?"

"He gave me disturbing news about my family … Oh, I wish your father were here."

"Tell me." Anya stamped her foot.

FORTY-TWO

Omsk 1920

ROMAN RESTED ON a wooden bench at the train station. It was a blustery cold day, and the train was late, a frequent occurrence. These days, one was lucky to see the train more than once a week. He pulled a letter from his breast pocket. He had tried to start it several days ago. This time, he was determined to get his thoughts on paper, if for nothing else than for posterity's sake.

> My beautiful darling,
>
> I don't know what plan fate has for me, but I want to express my deepest love for you and our darling daughter, who is almost a woman by now. I think of her often and hope she remembers her Papa. I am anguished over our time lost to the disruption of so many wars. I carry this letter with me. If I don't make it, my hope is that it will somehow find you.
>
> I don't wish to alarm you, but had it been

another time, I would have seen our daughter become a woman with children of her own, and we have grown old together. However, we may have missed our moment. My body aches with sadness.

Life is weary not hearing from you, and although we have been on the move so often, it would be impossible for your letters to reach me. My heart is filled with the fear of not seeing you again. I wonder how you are getting along in that strange, faraway city.

My dearest friend died in my arms. His loss wounds me to my marrow. I feel abandoned. My only salvation is reaching Shanghai. I hunger for your arms around me.

The army has collapsed. I admire the gaunt faces that remain with Kolchak but fear their loyalty may be for naught. Yesterday, we burned the ships along the river rather than leave them to the Reds. We are making our way to Irkutsk, where Kolchak transferred his headquarters. The snow is fast approaching, adding to the uncertainty of our journey. We hope to cross the Urals before a blizzard pours down on us. Once we reach Irkutsk, I plan to continue to Vladivostok and board a steamer to Shanghai. The days until then are filled with anguish.

I'm glad you're not here to see me. I have not bathed in weeks, and what is left of my uniform is covered in mud. With the untold numbers of workers and peasants who were shot, beaten, raped, and imprisoned, I wonder if I will ever forget the horror I have seen.

I leave you now in hopes of returning soon.

In the distance, a dark plume of locomotive smoke billowed high in the air. Roman folded the unfinished letter and returned it to his breast pocket. The army, those left, readied themselves to board. Anxieties were high, with rumors flying that Kolchak would relinquish his command with plans to escape the country. With all the dissatisfaction between the factions, Roman was surprised that Kolchak had evaded an assassination attempt.

WHEN THEY REACHED Irkutsk, it was clear that a revolutionary group, the Mensheviks, had seized power. Roman remembered the Menshevik riots that led to the Tsar's abdication from the throne. He held a deep disdain for them.

The roar of chaos consumed the area. Men were pulled off the train and asked where their loyalties lay. If they proclaimed allegiance to the Tsar, they were shot, and their bodies were thrown onto a cart. It only took a few to die before everyone pledged allegiance to Lenin, even Roman. He would have said anything to stay alive. But before they dragged him into their cause, he dashed into the station. He made his way through the crowd to the station clerk.

"When is the next train scheduled for Vladivostok?"

"Maybe tomorrow. Maybe next week," the clerk shrugged. "We never know when to expect it. You'll need to check daily."

"Thank you." Roman turned and headed for town. He wandered the streets aimlessly. People bumped into one another as if walking in a daze. Their faces showed no fear, yet they seemed to know something. *The culmination to the end of an era—perhaps?*

A man bumped into him with vigor. Roman was about to scold the man when he looked over and realized it was a fellow officer.

What are you doing here?" the officer grabbed Roman's arms and shook him. "I thought you'd be long gone."

"Waiting for a train," Roman said.

"Aren't we all?" He laughed. "I was sorry to hear about Uri. He was a damn good soldier."

Roman hung his head and nodded.

"Fancy a drink?"

"I'd prefer a bath and clean clothes first."

"No problem. I know just the place. And the women are friendly."

"Just a bath."

"Okay." He slapped Roman on the back.

ROMAN FELT RENEWED as he donned freshly laundered clothes for the first time in months. However, wearing civilian attire rather than a uniform felt oddly unfamiliar.

"How about that drink?"

"You read my mind," Roman said.

The two found solace in a rundown establishment,

a temporary refuge from the chaos outside. The straw beneath their feet had long decayed, filling the air with a musty smell. The tables and chairs they sat at wobbled from the uneven ground. A testament to the situation.

"Your finest vodka barkeep," the officer ordered. He nudged Roman. "It's probably some homemade rotgut."

Roman smiled. "At this point, I'd take anything."

"Did you hear that Kolchak placed himself under allied protection?

"No."

"The Czechs handed him over to the Bolsheviks for their safe passage to the Far East."

"Where were his bodyguards?"

"They deserted him."

"I knew not to trust those Czech devils."

"They are hunting for Kolchak's officers. Lenin fears another uprising if he doesn't kill us all."

"God, I hope that train comes tomorrow."

The officer lifted his glass. "To leaving this hell for another."

FORTY-THREE
Shanghai

A GENTLE KNOCK was heard at the door. "Who could be calling on us at this time of night? Kira addressed Anya. Kira opened the door and saw a brown-eyed boy in a blue uniform holding an envelope.

"Mrs. Pavlich?" The boy tipped his cap.

"Pavlovitch," Kira nodded.

"Telegram, Madam." He handed her the envelope and left.

What if it's word that Roman is dead? Her hands shook as she tore open the envelope and read the heading. Kira crumpled the telegram and clutched her chest.

"What is it, Mother?"

"It's from my father." She exhaled a sigh. Kira unrumpled the message and continued to read it aloud. "He received our address from the French

Council. You see, dear, that's why I met the Baron. It was his doing."

Anya recoiled with a guttural sound.

"They are in Calais, waiting to go to England and perhaps on to America. They heard that the Bolsheviks were in control of the Urals and planned to unite every city from St. Petersburg to Vladivostok."

Kira looked up and smiled at Anya. "This means that your father will be with us soon."

"That's wonderful news, Mother. What else does he say?"

"Let's see." She read the following line and felt her legs give way as she sank into a nearby chair.

"What?" Anya said with a hushed squawk.

Kira's voice shook. "Your aunt Catherine has died." Her stomach ached as if someone had punched it. Her hand relaxed. The telegram floated to the floor.

Kira remembered the last time she saw her sister and how frail and gaunt she looked in bed. She believed Catherine no longer held the will to live with the loss of her fiancée and died of a broken heart.

Anya handed her a handkerchief.

"I refused to cry. I am sick of the grief, the loss, the endless heartache. All I have left is anger."

"Don't be angry, Mama."

"I'll be alright, dear." Kira took the handkerchief. She thought about the times she and her sister would play tricks on the younger siblings, they being five and eight years apart. They would hide a favorite toy and tell them Mother had thrown it away. Only to have Mother scold the two for playing such a nasty trick and send them to bed without supper. She recalled the many formal events they attended. They would spend the entire day giddy and excited, preening and fixing one another's hair. Knowing that not one man attending was worth their time. However, not all parties were in vain. At one such event, Catherine met a wealthy businessman who danced her heart away. Unfortunately, he died in a factory accident, leaving her sister heartbroken and vowing never to marry. But that had only lasted until she met her lieutenant. After hearing of his death in the war, Kira prayed she would find joy again. She desperately wanted Catherine to experience the happiness and love that she and Roman shared.

Kira became aware of her surroundings. "I feel your eyes on me, dear. What else is said?"

Anya picked up the message. "They hope the boat will come soon as food and water are scarce with so many refugees. They wish us all well and hope one day we can be together."

"Not all of us," Kira muttered, her words hung in the air.

THE FOLLOWING DAY, Kira received an invitation from the Baron. *I don't wish to see him, but I feel obligated to thank him for his help. I'll tell him my husband will be returning and I can't stay.* She crumpled the message and threw it in the wastebasket. She didn't want Anya to find it and lecture her about meeting him.

Before Kira left the hired cab, the driver asked her if this was the right place. She responded with certainty. A sweet, musty smell hit her as she walked into the place. Heavy drapes covered the windows, casting the room in a dim light. A man fingered a sultry tune on the piano. The room was arranged in an intimate setting with various couples in deep conversation.

She felt a presence near her.

"Good day."

She twirled around to see the Baron. He was dressed in a black shirt and white tie. *He looks like a gangster right off the silver screen.* She suddenly felt vulnerable and, for the first time, a bit unsure of herself. *I should have headed the taxicab driver's caution.*

She started to speak, but he interrupted her.

"Come. Let's have a drink."

"I can't stay. I just wanted to thank you for your help. My father contacted me."

"Please. I insist." He flagged over a server and ordered two champagnes.

"None for me. I must return home. My husband

will be arriving any day now. I must make sure the house is ready in time." She wasn't sure what words streamed from her mouth.

He caressed her shoulder.

Kira pulled away.

The server arrived with the drinks. The Baron handed her a glass.

She refused.

"You must have known it would come to this. A married woman does not meet a man unescorted if they wish to remain respectable," he said.

She slapped him and then again. She was used to men falling in love with her and had always used it to her advantage. She remembered Uri was very attentive while Roman was away. But he had always been a gentleman. Her eyes were now open to this brute, this monster, this charlatan.

"You aristocratic women think you can toy with men's affections without repercussions." He grabbed Kira by her upper arm and pulled her toward him in an attempt to kiss her.

Kira struggled to free herself. From behind, she heard a familiar voice.

"Let go of my mother this instant."

Kira stood frozen. "How?" She turned to see not just a daughter but a forceful presence.

"I found the note and followed you here," Anya said.

"Who is this little one?" the Baron released his grip.

"My brave daughter." Kira embraced Anya.

The room had gone silent. All eyes were on them, waiting for their next move.

"Come, Mother." Anya took her mother's arm and escorted her out.

The Baron did not follow.

Once outside, Kira stopped. "Anya, you mustn't tell your father about this. Promise me."

"It will be our secret. I'm very good at keeping secrets."

FORTY-FOUR

Irkutsk

THE TRAIN FAILED to arrive the next day, and there was no assurance when it would come. Roman's shoulders slumped, and his knees weakened as if forces were pulling him to the ground. Knowing that the Bolshevik army was in control west of the Urals and on the move to Irkutsk, he felt the pressure to press on—by foot if necessary.

Roman heard of a massive party numbering over 20,000 strong, including women and children, who were embarking on a daunting trek over mountainous terrain to Chita. After weighing all the alternatives, He decided it was the worthiest of options. Safety in numbers, he reasoned, was the better risk.

Winter had begun to tighten its grip, promising to become more brutal. Roman knew he was about to tackle bone-chilling wind and ice. He purchased oversized boots, several pairs of socks, gloves, a long wool coat, and a fur hat with the money he had left. There would be funds at the house in Vladivostok—if he could make it through the unforgiving trek.

Roman said goodbye to the officer he had befriended. The officer planned to go through Mongolia and China to reach India. He told Roman it was a place he always wanted to visit.

THE GROUP HEADED east and followed the train tracks until they reached Lake Baikal. His mind snapped back to when the family had picnicked along the lakeside when they moved to Vladivostok. He hesitated, but crossing the frozen lake would save time and possibly his life.

The treacherous walk provided a uniquely serene vista. Roman stood in the middle of the frozen lake. A cloudless azure sky accentuated the surrounding virgin green forest. He saw shiny stones and fish swimming under the clear ice in one particular place.

Icicles hung from Roman's long facial hair. Even though he was dressed in protective clothing, he still felt the sting of the ferocious arctic winds as they blew unobstructed across the lake, causing burning pins and needles of numbness in his fingers and toes.

An elderly couple stumbled ahead. Roman tried to assist, but the man insisted on resting.

"Only for a moment," he said.

"If you stay too long, you will freeze to death," Roman said.

"We will be alright."

Roman saw the despair in the man's eyes. That and the forlorn expression on the woman's face and her blue lips said it all. Roman barely had the strength to continue, let alone carry someone. His stomach twisted, knowing their destiny.

Frozen corpses littered the lake. Grayish-yellow-colored families lay huddled on the ice, with babies nuzzled in their mother's arms. To Roman, it appeared as though they had fallen asleep. He knew that come spring thaw, they would vanish into the deep lake water.

Those who survived the crossing continued through a mountainous region. Fortune was with them as the snowfall was light that season. Men with rifles hunted for deer and bighorn sheep, sharing their kill with the survivors.

Roman struggled with the night hours. He feared sleep—the chance he might not wake. An aura of wavy, luminescent green lights danced in the sky. The lights seemed to calm him as he drifted into dreamland. Each morning, he awoke grateful to be alive with the promise of seeing Kira and Anya.

BY THE TIME they reached Chita, the group, which had embarked on a daring journey, was half its original size. The area seemed familiar to Roman. He suddenly remembered it was nearby where his brother and fellow outlaws robbed the train from Port Arthur. He recalled him recovering from a wound inflicted by an Imperial Guard's sword. Roman chuckled to himself and wondered how his rascal brother was getting on.

The region was controlled by Kolchak's successor and supported by the Japanese military. Most of the survivors stayed, but Roman continued east. A scheduled train ran between Chita and Vladivostok, but he had no money. He wished he had his uniform, which would have provide him a free ride. Many gave up their uniforms for fear of being confronted by revolutionaries or no longer wanting an affiliation with the Tsar.

Wandering the streets, he stumbled upon a surplus store. Luck would again be with him. He was able to trade his fur coat and hat for a uniform. He selected a low-ranking officer's uniform to ensure anonymity.

Roman boarded the train and sat alone in a coach compartment. For the first time in months, he felt the promise of hope that he would unite with his family. The moment was fleeting when a strange little man with a broad face, high cheekbones, and dark complexion approached. Roman knew from experience that he was of Mongolian descent. The man held a tight grip on an elaborate silver-capped cane. But he had no sign of a limp. The glint in his eyes and crooked smile unnerved Roman. The man gave him a determined stare as he passed the compartment.

Ahead, Roman spotted the conductor punching tickets. His palms moistened, and his heart pounded.

What if he asks for my papers? When the conductor reached Roman's compartment, his hands shook. His mind reeled as he held his breath with anticipation. The conductor tipped his hat and walked on. Roman exhaled, releasing the tension. He rested his head on the back of the bench and closed his eyes.

Moments later, his stomach grumbled. *When did I last have a meal?* He made his way to the dining car. A band of rowdy soldiers enjoyed themselves with a spread of various meats and cheeses. And the usual libation, vodka. At the end of the car sat the little man with the same glint and smile. Roman joined the soldiers, who were happy to include a fellow compadre.

As the evening progressed, Roman was aware of that strange man's attentiveness. After several shots, he decided to confront him. He grabbed his glass, nabbed a bottle, and plopped across from him.

"You seem to know me, sir," Roman said.

"You remind me of an officer I once met. Major Roman Pavlovitch." He spoke with a slither that seeps across the tongue when one is lying. "The name's Sun … Sun Temujin." He rubbed the silver tip of his cane.

Roman could not recall having met the man. Though worse for drink, he was suspicious and refused to concede anything. *What kind of a man dresses like a Christmas package in a tight-fitting, double-breasted suit, patterned necktie, and carries a fancy cane.* He gulped from his glass. "Well … I don't know you, so you couldn't possibly know me."

"He served under Kolchak." His tone was venomous. "I wanted to convey my condolences. I understand the admiral was murdered and his body dumped in the river."

Roman sensed a burning fire start to rise from inside but refused to challenge him. Instead, remained straight-faced. "I'm sorry, but you have me confused with someone else." He rose to leave but could sense Sun's pursuant eyes, his suspicion growing stronger with each step.

ROMAN ARRIVED IN Vladivostok to find the Japanese in command of the area. Although he hadn't seen Sun since their last encounter, he couldn't shake off the feeling of his eerie presence, a mystery that lingered in the air.

He entered the family house. Melancholy surrounded his thoughts as his footsteps reverberated across the wooden floor. The stark room contained his favorite dilapidated, overstuffed chair positioned next to the picture window as though waiting for him.

A bittersweet smile spread across Roman's face as he relaxed in the chair. He closed his eyes and remembered Anya's first Christmas, a time when a young child could fully appreciate the wonder and excitement such a holiday brings. She had ripped open a wrapped package to find a Steiff teddy bear with a red bow tied around its neck. The joy on her face had filled him with pride. And he loved that it had remained a prize possession of hers. *It's in Shanghai, keeping watch over my baby girl.*

Roman opened his eyes and set his sights on the wharf below. *I better get down there and make arrangements for passage.* He forced open a floorboard and pulled out a satchel. Not knowing the outcome of the political future, he had always kept a supply of yens, rubles, and francs in it.

ROMAN REACHED THE harbor to find a flurry of people desperate to book passage—anywhere. Cargo carriers, liners, and cruisers were docked or anchored in the harbor. They displayed flags from Japan, China, Britain, and America. He made his way to the ticket office. Long lines of people clutching their possessions and children's hands filled the room. When he reached the ticket counter, he was told that all passage liners were sold out. He purchased a ticket on a Chinese container ship that would take several weeks. However, it departed the following day.

Roman looked up from his ticket and spotted Sun lurking in the shadows. A chill ran through him. *Why is this man stalking me? I sense he wishes me harm.* In an instant, he knew he had to elude Sun. Unable to blend into the crowd, as he towered over most, he struggled against the tsunami mob. He found an opening and quickly made his way to a warehouse. In his haste, he knocked over a rickshaw. The owner screamed and swore at him, but Roman could not stop to apologize.

Dashing into the warehouse, he hid behind a stack of wooden pallets. Spying through the pallets slits, he waited to see if Sun had followed him.

Roman overheard Chinese loaders complaining about having to finish loading a cargo ship as it was to leave that evening. When he believed he had evaded Sun, he approached the men and spoke to them in Mandarin. "Where is the ship docked?" One man pointed straight ahead. Roman thanked him. *Hopefully, Sun will believe I'm sailing on the other liner tomorrow if I can get on this ship.*

A Japanese officer stood at the foot of the loading platform. Roman walked over to him and offered him a bribe to board. The officer looked him over and then agreed. The voyage would take a week to arrive in Shanghai. Once on board and out of sight, Roman surveyed the area to see if Sun crept about. *I think I've dodged him.* Every muscle in his body relaxed, and he exhaled a sigh of freedom.

The bribe may have worked, but he still had to work for his passage. The officer assigned him the job of shoveling coal into the boiler. The physical toll was immense. To maintain a consistent feeding of the furnace, one man would feed the blazing incinerator while the other gasped for the air pipe funneled in from outside. Each man took turns catching breaths of fresh air until it was his turn to feed the fire. The intense heat and stifling air caused Roman to occasionally gasp for breaths. But his greater fear was a stroke or mere insanity. He now understood the stories of stokers who jumped overboard before the ship docked. By the end of the day, his clothes were covered in soot. Roman showered with his clothes on and slept in them wet. It was a way to reduce his internal body heat until the next shift.

The only thing that kept him going was his goal of reaching his family. He would be in Shanghai the next day.

FORTY-FIVE
Shanghai

ROMAN RESTED HIS forearms against the cold steel railing and looked ahead with anticipation as the steamship propelled around the final bend of the Huangpu River. His heartbeat quickened at the sight of Shanghai's port. The glorious eclectic architecture and bustling promenade brought tears to his eyes. *I've finally arrived.*

When his feet touched land, his sea legs wobbled as though he were still onboard. He put one leg before the other and walked forcefully until he regained equilibrium. He turned a corner onto a busy avenue. His senses were overwhelmed by the familiar sights of a vodka distillery, Russian sable furrier, Stepanoff jewelry, and the fragrant smells wafting from the Tkachenko restaurant and a Russian bakery. A chill ran through him. *It feels like home—almost.*

Roman questioned threatening signs: No Chinese Permitted on these Premises and Whites Only bathrooms. He had not experienced this type of discrimination in Vladivostok. Two European men approached, then quickly skidded away from him with a look of disdain. As they passed, he heard them say coolies. *What's a coolie? A new drink? He* shook it off.

Roman had no way of notifying Kira when he would arrive. And no idea where she lived. However, he did have Chiu's address. With what money he had left, he hired a two-wheeled rickshaw.

Roman disembarked in front of a newspaper shop and walked into the building. A Chinese woman greeted him with a bow, which he reciprocated.

Roman spoke to her in as much Mandarin as he could muster. "I am looking for Monsieur. Chiu."

She covered her mouth and giggled, then pointed to a door at the end of the hall.

He bowed and thanked her.

Roman knocked at the door but waited to hear the word enter before he opened it. Chiu sat at his desk, scouring over papers. "Monsieur Chiu, I am Roman Pavolvitch," Chiu looked up. "I know we have never met formally, but I have recently arrived in Shanghai."

Chiu jumped from his seat and vigorously shook Roman's hand. "I am so happy to meet you at last."

Roman saw the grim look on Chiu's face. "I apologize for my appearance." He brushed his grubby attire.

"Would you care for some tea?" Chiu yelled out to the woman to bring tea.

Roman looked at him sheepishly.

"I suppose you are anxious to see your wife and child?" Chiu smiled.

"Yes. Can you take me there?"

"With pleasure. Come." Chiu waved Roman forward, then stopped and looked him up and down. "Maybe we should get you cleaned up first."

"Yes," Roman chuckled. "That would be best."

The woman rushed down the hall with the tea. Chiu brushed her aside. "We have no time for that now."

CHIU STOPPED THE car in front of a pristine white stucco building. "It's on the third floor." He pointed.

Roman sat paralyzed, his heart pounding. *I have thought so long and hard about this moment. Why has fear suddenly crept in?*

"Do you want me to go up with you?" Chiu said.

"No. I'll be alright." Roman's trembling hand slowly reached for the door handle. He stepped onto the sidewalk and stared at the third-floor window. He adjusted his new jacket, inhaled a deep breath and exhaled.

So much time has passed ... almost two years. Roman climbed the flights of stairs with trepidation. "Will they recognize me? Will they judge me? Will they accept me? What if they don't?" He stopped at the landing and hesitated at the door before knocking. There was no answer. He knocked again. He heard Kira's voice through the door.

"Coming. Coming." Kira opened the door wearing an apron and a dishrag in her hand. She stood still for a split second. Her eyes welled up, and she started to shake. The cloth dropped to the floor and she jumped into Roman's arms.

They embraced with warm kisses at the doorway until Kira pulled him in. Her face flushed as she tried to reposition loose strands of hair. "I must look a mess."

"You look beautiful."

Kira picked up the dishrag and straitened magazines on the side table. Her movements were awkward. "Can I get you anything?" A quiver rose in her voice. "Water, coffee, tea, vodka?"

"I think we could both use a drink."

Kira excused herself and went into the kitchen.

Roman scanned the room. He called out. "Where is Anya?"

Kira entered the room with a bottle of vodka and two glasses. "She's at church feeding the unfortunate ones."

"Unfortunate ones?"

Kira filled the glasses and handed one to Roman. She lifted her glass and said, "*Venir chez toi.*"

They sat on the davenport. "Anya has become a crusader for the Russian refugees pouring into the city.

I'm very proud of her but concerned she may be taking it to an extreme."

"How?"

"She has been depleting our food supplies to the point where I feel the need to stand in line at the church to get a decent meal."

They both laughed.

"The refugee situation has escalated into a dire crisis. With most refugees not speaking English, the common trade language, making their employment opportunities limited. This has led to a burden on the city and caused hostility among the Chinese population. The newly formed League of Nations has made efforts to assist, but with their limited funds, the situation remains critical. The majority of refugees are too impoverished to afford transportation to other countries, and many nations are unwilling to accept them." Kira paused. "I believe this is largely due to their Jewish identity."

Roman stared into Kira's eyes. "God, you are as beautiful as the day I saw you glide across the palace floor in St. Petersburg." He took her in his arms and drew her close.

The jiggle of the font door knob diverted their attention. Anya stepped into the room. Frozen in her footsteps, her hand remaining on the knob.

Roman stood up to greet his daughter. He was taken aback by the dramatic transformation in her appearance. *The skinny little girl I left is a young lady with plump cheeks and a woman's silhouette.*

"Papa, you're home. You're home. You're Home. And in time for my birthday." She wrapped her arms around his waist and buried her face in his chest.

He pulled her away to get a better look. "What happened to my little girl? And your beautiful long auburn hair. What have you done?"

"Oh, Papa. I had to grow up sometime." She sashayed around the room.

"Kira, how could you allow it?" He gave her a wink.

Kira shrugged. "She is a young woman with a mind of her own."

"Anyway, short hair or no hair. It's just good to be together." He embraced them both.

KIRA SET A breakfast plate of blinis in front of Roman. She sat at the table and folded her arms on her midriff. "Now that we are   a family again, we must discuss Anya's future."

Roman indulged in a hearty helping of pancake. "So soon…" he swallowed. "I don't see the necessity."

"She will be eighteen. It's crucial that we carefully consider her proper introduction into society," Kira stated with unwavering determination.

"He laughed but quickly closed his mouth at the sight of Kira's furrowed brow. "Kira, I'm afraid those days have vanished."

Kira stood. "More coffee?"

Roman nodded and admired his wife's form as she approached the stove.

"I have been looking into a finishing school in Switzerland. I believe it will provide her with a proper education and wonderful opportunities. She poured coffee into Roman's empty cup.

"Can you afford to have her away from you that long? The both of you have come to rely on each other."

"Yes, but…it's better for her."

"But what of the expense?"

"With all the traveling, moving, and the cost to live, my dowry has dwindled. But there is good work here for those who are willing."

"Let's hold off on any future decisions about Anya until we have a better outlook on our permanent living situation."

SEVERAL DAYS LATER, as the last rays of the sunset reflected through a slit in the drapes, Roman and Kira prepared for Anya's birthday celebration. They had made arrangements for a lavish gathering that included the Chiu family.

"Where is Anya?" Roman said as he slid his black trousers on.

"She's with Bia, dressing for the party." Kira stepped into her tight-fitting beaded gown and shimmied it over her slender frame. "Today, girls do each other's hair and face powder. Makeup, they call it."

"I'm not sure I condone such behavior." He tucked in his white shirt.

"Finishing school, darling."

"You may be right." He knotted his tie.

"Can you button me up?" Kira turned her back to him. The glimmer of the ring on the dresser caught her eye. "Oh dear, Anya has forgotten her Fabergé ring. I'll take it for her tonight."

He zipped up the dress and kissed the nape of her neck.

She turned to face him, adjusted his tie, and looked into his eyes. "I am so grateful we are all together again."

"Even though we are without a country."

She smiled. "After all these years, our love and devotion to family will always endure wherever we dwell."

About the Author

P. C. Chinick, a traditionally fiction thriller writer, is now embarking on a new journey with *Roman and Kira*, a romance saga. This transition comes after the success of the Red Asscher series, *Living in Fear,* which received a Gold medal for the best thriller from Global Ebook Awards, a Silver from BellaOnline, and was a Winner for *Scintillating Starts* from the online magazine Writer Advice.